I0846892

One Hundred Saints

Yolanda Olson

Copyright

Copyright © 2016 Yolanda Olson

All rights reserved. No part of this publication may be reproduced, distributed, or transmitted in any form, or by any means, including photocopying, recording, or other electronic or mechanical methods, without the prior written permission from the author, except in the case of brief quotations embodied in critical reviews and certain other noncommercial uses permitted by copyright law. This book is a work of fiction. Names, characters, places, and incidents are products of the author's imagination or are used fictitiously. Any resemblance to actual events, locales, or persons living or dead, is entirely coincidental.

Revised 2nd Edition © 2024

Edited & Formatted by Ally Vance Author Services

Blurb

He was from the wrong side of the bayou.

A place where voodoo was revered and fallen angels whispered.

I didn't care.

I loved him from the first time we played together, and I love him still.

I haven't seen him in so long.

I went back to New Orleans when I could.

I never stopped thinking about him.

My bayou boy with the heavy Cajun accent.

I just didn't know that the happy little boy had turned into such a different man.

I didn't know that he had been looking for me too.

I didn't know a lot of things.

But finding out was much worse than staying in the dark.

Prologue

(When We Were Young)

"Hey, Grimm!" I called out happily.

The boy who couldn't have been more than two years older than me, turned slightly to see who was greeting him. He moved away from the tree he had been thoughtfully leaning against, and dug his hands into his pockets, a small smile curving the corners of his lips.

"Hi, Miss Emily," he called back to me.

"I told you not to call me that," I chided, giving him a quick hug. "Emmie will do just fine, thank you very much."

He rested his cheek on the top of my head for a moment, before he nodded and pulled away. I liked Grimm for a lot of reasons, but I always felt like his hugs weren't something he really wanted to give to anyone. Sometimes, his hugs reminded me of a robot that was trying to learn how to feel things; emotions, I guess.

It was a beautiful, hot summer day so I knew I would find him fishing the Mississippi River over in Old Algiers. I also had a present for him, and I knew I would have to convince him to follow me home to be able to give it to him.

He took my hand and led me to our favorite spot near the tree he loved so much, and sat down on the grass, pulling me down beside him. I reached down and smoothed out the bottom of my skirt, while he brought his legs up and wrapped his arms around his knees, watching me.

"You always wear fancy clothes, Emmie?" he asked curiously.

"This? This isn't fancy! It's a secondhand buy from the thrift shop over on St. Charles Avenue," I replied with a dismissive laugh.

Grimm scoffed and turned his eyes back toward his fishing pole. I immediately felt bad, because I was pretty sure that the only pants he owned in the entire world were the ones he wore every day. It made me wonder about his parents; if he had any, and if they even cared. He never liked to talk about himself, but he would spend hours on end listening to me go on and on about Daddy, Mama, and Mr. and Mrs. Rourke.

That's why today I was especially excited to see him; 'cause of the present I had for him.

"When was the last time you ate something?" I asked, poking at his ribs.

"The last time I caught a fish," he replied with a shrug.

I turned my eyes toward the river for a moment, trying to recall when that was. If it had been when I was with him—and it had to, because I spent almost every day with him for the past three weeks—that meant it was two days ago.

"Grimm Valot, why didn't you tell me that yesterday?" I asked angrily. "I woulda took you home with me, and Mrs. Rourke coulda made you supper!"

He shook his head, but he didn't say anything. It was obvious that Grimm wasn't going to make accepting my offer easy; he'd probably see it as an act of charity when it really wasn't.

"You wanna know something? You're my very best friend in the world," I admitted softly.

"I don't believe that for one moment, Emily Thibideaux. You *must* have better friends than me," he said, picking up a pebble and tossing it in the water.

"It's true! You're the only friend who actually listens when I talk. You make me feel better when I feel like crying, just by sitting here with me," I insisted, looking at him.

He grunted and threw another pebble into the river. I sighed unhappily. I wanted him to feel better about himself by admitting he was my best friend, and it only seemed to put him in a sour mood instead.

"I have a present for you!" I said brightly. Grimm gave me a sideward glance and raised his eyebrows.

"What is it?" he finally asked after staring at me for a moment.

"You gotta come to my house so I can give it you," I replied with a smile.

He let out a laugh as he got to his feet and went to check his line. When he was sure that he hadn't caught anything yet, he turned around and crossed his arms over his bare, dirty chest.

"Emmie, you know good and well that your Pa isn't gonna let me come into your house. Neither is your Ma. No matter how much you ask them, they won't let me come in, and you know why? Because you come from a completely different place than I do. I see it, your Ma and Pa see it; you're the only one who doesn't see it," he replied, shaking his head vehemently.

I hopped up and walked over to where he was standing. I really wanted to push him into the river for being such a blockhead. I put one hand on my hip and pointed a finger in his face.

"Don't you dare tell me what I see and don't see, because if you knew, you wouldn't want so badly to make me not want to be your friend anymore. You can't get rid of me until I wanna go away, and I'm not going anywhere. So, you can stop being mean to me and just come to my house tonight!" I shouted, stomping my foot on the soft grass.

His eyes widened briefly, and then his shoulders slumped. He reached forward and pulled me into a tight hug so I wouldn't be angry anymore.

"Why are you so good to me, Emmie?" he asked into my hair.

"Because someone has to show you what a good person you are. I love you, Grimm and I always will. I'll never want or find another best friend like you," I replied, gripping him tightly.

"I love you too, Emmie. I know I don't say it as much as I should, but I do. You're my best and only friend," he said quietly.

I pulled back and looked up into his big, blue eyes. It was the right time to make him promise to come to my house, which he finally agreed to do. I knew that Daddy and Mama would see what I saw; they would see past the dirty boy with the torn clothes and the stern face.

They'd see someone who was destined for great things, and they would love him because I did. I told Grimm to meet me at my house around nine o'clock that night and to come through the gardens. I wanted to play him the song I wrote for him first—his present—then I would introduce my very best friend to my parents.

I couldn't wait to see what would come of it. Maybe they'd let us play in the garden together and maybe they'd have Mrs. Rourke make him supper.

After all, what was the worst that could happen?

The French Quarter

One

Daddy's driver was slowly rounding the corner from the house my parents lived in. I hadn't seen them in a couple of years, and they didn't know I was coming. I didn't have anything against my parents, and they didn't have anything against me; we just decided to take a break from each other. Kind of like one of those volatile relationships where everyone needs a breather before regrouping.

My daddy was a smart man; he made his money in construction and was one of the first companies that offered to help rebuild the levees in the Lower Ninth Ward. They turned him away though; told him it was too dangerous for anyone to go out there.

Mama was as good a woman as daddy

was smart. She was a classic beauty, reminding me of a modern-day Scarlett O'Hara–with her curly brown hair, and her distant brown eyes looking as if she was lost in a daydream.

I took after her in basic looks, though I was slightly larger than her. Slender but not slim, whereas Daddy was a tall man with reddish brown hair and big blue eyes. My brother looked so much like him that they could have been twins if Daddy were younger.

"We're here, Miss Emmie," the driver said, bringing the sleek black Rolls Royce to a stop.

I leaned toward the window and glanced up at the two-story structure and sighed. "Indeed we are."

I waited while he got out of the driver's seat and walked around the side of the car to open my door.

"It's good to see you again," he said, tipping his hat to me once I was standing next to him.

I smiled at Mr. Rourke. He had been the family's driver for as long as I could remember, and he always had a kind word for everyone. He was an older man with the leatheriest skin I had ever seen in my life, but kind blue eyes, and a big heart.

I reached up and put my arms around his shoulders, giving him a firm hug before we pulled apart and he handed me my rolling bag. With a wave, I left him standing next to the car as I walked toward the front door of my parents' home.

Down the street I heard some children laughing as I raised my fist to knock on the door. A few moments later, they were running past me like they had a fire lit underneath them.

I laughed and raised my hand to knock again when Mrs. Rourke pulled the door open slightly.

"Hi!" I said brightly, with a big smile on

my face.

"Oh my goodness!" she said, rushing forward to sweep me up in her arms. "Miss Emmie, I can't believe it's really you!"

She was a pleasant older woman with a stocky body, shorter than me by a head, and her hair was neatly tied up the same tight white bun I had always seen since childhood.

"Your parents will be so happy to see you!" she exclaimed.

I swallowed the nervous lump that had been rising in my throat and nodded. Maybe they would be and maybe they wouldn't be; I wouldn't know for sure until I actually stepped into the house. "Go on into the parlor and I'll let them know you're here."

"Thanks Maggie," I replied softly.

I waited a few moments, glued to where I was, as I watched her head off to find Mama and Daddy. I bit my lip nervously and decided to finally walk down to the parlor, the wheels on my bag making a muffled rolling sound as I dragged it behind me down the carpeted hallway. I knew that if I left any tracks behind from it that Maggie would take care of it, and Mama would never know.

It wasn't a far walk from the front door of the house to the glass double doors of the parlor. A slight hesitation came over me as I put a hand on the brass handle, and I wondered if I should leave and call them instead. I could tell them that I had just arrived in town and that I wanted to come see them, if they had the time for me.

Maggie has probably found them by now, I thought to myself, pulling open the right-hand door. One step inside and I instantly smiled. The room looked as brand new as the day that Daddy had added it into the house. Just inside the doors and to the right, was a large wicker chair that Mama had bought at one of the markets in town. It had been one of my favorite things in the entire house, and as I propped my bag against it, I was happy to see that she still had it.

I glanced around the room quickly and

let out a happy squeal when I saw the beautiful grand piano that I had spent so many hot Louisiana summer nights playing, sitting in the far back, left-hand corner of the room.

I went over and sat down on the bench, lifting the cover off of the ivory keys, and running my fingers gently across them. With a happy sigh, I thought of the last time Daddy had allowed me to play in this room alone. He had heard the sounds of a song that had just come to me; a hauntingly beautiful melody he called it, something to light fires to and chase away the spirits. It was a song that reminded me of my good friend, Grimm, and I had snuck him into the parlor so I could play the tune for him. I think it was the only time I had ever seen him smile. Even when Daddy came in and angrily chased him out of the house and through the gardens, I'd like to think the smile never left his face.

Grimm was a big reason I had come back to New Orleans. Honestly, he was the main reason I had come back. Ever since Hurricane

Katrina had swept through and destroyed the Lower Ninth Ward—where he lived with his family—I worried that they hadn't made it; that *he* hadn't made it.

It would break my heart to find out he was dead, because he was my very best friend. Days spent sitting on the grass and watching him throw his line into the Mississippi River always made me happy. I would sit for hours and watch him fish, and there were even times where, even after the sun went down, we would sit behind the trees so no one could see us, and just talk.

I had never known Grimm to smile; not until that day he sat with me while I played my song for him. I sighed and glanced at the wicker chair again. The reason it was my favorite piece of furniture in the entire house was because that was the only place he had felt safe enough to sit. It put him within sightline of both sets of doors in case he needed to run, he had said.

"Emily!" Daddy said happily as he entered the room.

And I didn't even get to play the entire song for him before you chased him away, I thought sadly as I got to my feet and walked over to him.

"Hi, Daddy," I replied softly as we hugged each other. Mama entered the room a moment later with a big smile on her face.

"Why didn't you tell us you were coming?" she asked, with a big smile and outstretched arms.

"Hi, Mama," I said, letting her wrap me up in her arms for a tight hug. *You didn't stop him. You always followed him into rooms, and you still didn't stop him from chasing away my friend,* I thought, pulling away from her.

"Sit, sit, sit," Daddy said, as he and Mama took their usual spots in the parlor. He sat in the huge leather chair by the fireplace and Mama sat in the maple colored rocking chair next to him. I went back to the piano bench and sat down, pulling one leg underneath myself, and wondered what to say. I hadn't thought this far ahead.

"How long has it been?" Mama asked me as she rested a hand on Daddy's arm.

"I don't really know; maybe three or four years?" I replied, tilting my head to the left. "Four. It's been four."

"And what brings you home?" Daddy asked curiously. "It's not Mardi Gras, is it?"

I rolled my eyes, even though I didn't mean to. I knew it was rude and disrespectful, but my parents were very religious and conservative and didn't like the whole idea of Mardi Gras.

"No, Daddy," I replied with a long-suffering sigh. "I didn't come to 'indulge in the sin for twenty four hours and then pray it away the next day.'" It was his favorite saying when it came to Mardi Gras, and I wanted him to be sure I hadn't forgotten it.

"I know you didn't come just to see us, did you?" he asked curiously, glancing at Mama.

"No, Daddy," I said softly.

"So, why are you here?" Mama pressed.

At that point it was starting to feel like an interrogation instead of a small family reunion, and I found myself wondering if I should have even bothered to stop in on them. But I wasn't going to give up my reason to them for being here; not yet.

"It had better not be to see that boy," Daddy warned in a stern voice.

"He's not a boy anymore, and I'm not a little girl either! You can't keep me from my friends, Daddy," I shot back.

Mama sighed loudly as Daddy got to his feet. I met her sigh as I stood up and went over to get my bag. Once Daddy stood up in anger, it meant any conversation he was having was over.

"It was nice to see you," he said, stepping out of the parlor and nodding toward the front door.

I stopped in front of him, but he wouldn't meet my eyes, and I felt a small sadness growing inside of me.

"I love you, Daddy," I said softly, before he turned on his heel and went back into the parlor.

Two

As soon as I told Daddy I was looking for Grimm, he all but opened the door and shoved me out. I never really knew what he had against him or his family, other than they were poor and we weren't. It wasn't fair, and I hated that living a life of privilege was supposed to mean that everyone else was beneath me. I never saw it like that.

I was walking down the streets toward the markets, my bag rolling noisily behind me on the rubble, thinking some shopping therapy was needed. I would be able to buy some fresh fruits from the locals and help them feed their families. It would also give me a chance to ask questions about the Lower Ninth Quarter since I had no way of getting there. Parts of it were still sectioned off and no one was allowed to go there, but someone had to know *something*.

When I heard the bustle and sounds of loud voices drifting toward me, I stopped walking and opened my bag to retrieve my wallet. I loved the markets in New Orleans, but the pickpockets were skilled, and I had a fairly large amount of cash in mine. Once I wrapped the strap firmly around my wrist, I zipped up my bag again and made my way toward the small, lively area near the river. It was hotter there and the bugs from the river were drifting toward everything, but I was happily looking at the fresh fruits from the first stand I had wandered closest too.

Mm. Pineapples, I thought, my stomach suddenly rumbling with hunger. The man behind the stand came over to me with a plastic bag. I asked him how much he was selling them for, and he said they were two dollars each. I bought two and handed him a twenty dollar bill. He reached into his pocket to give me change, but one glance around his almost full stand and I waved it off.

"What's your name?" I asked him.

"Monroe," he replied in a bayou accent I knew too well. "Thank you for this, Miss."

The people here were always so kind, and I hated to know that any of them struggled in any way. I knew if I didn't do something about at least one of them, I'd probably lose sleep over it tonight.

"My name is Emily St. Martin. Tonight before you go home, I want you to stop by the butcher's shop in town. Can you do that for me, Monroe?" I asked, putting a hand on his frail, thin wrist. I used my Mama's maiden name, just to be on the safe side.

His golden brown eyes brimmed with tears and he nodded his head once. The beige fishing hat that sat on top of his head was as worn as his beautiful brown skin, and I knew it was from working as hard as he did.

Before I turned to go, I glanced around for a moment. "Monroe, do you know anything about the Lower Ninth Quarter?"

"A little bit, Miss Emily," he said, moving back behind his stand. "What's a girl like you want with that place?"

I sighed deeply. I wasn't even sure what I wanted; if Grimm was still alive, I wouldn't go see him because it was too dangerous. If he wasn't alive, I would be completely heartbroken. I wasn't sure what to do anymore and it hadn't even been a full day yet.

"I had a friend who lived there before Katrina went through and destroyed it. Just wondering if there's any chance he might still be alive," I said quietly.

"I don't know, Miss Emily. I wouldn't count on it though," Monroe said woefully, shaking his head. "Here. You leave that bag with me while you go around the market. My son will be here soon, and he'll make sure nothing happens to it."

I smiled at him and let him take my lone

luggage bag from me and hide it behind his stand. I liked him, but being too trusting was a fault I had, and freely admitted to, and something Mama and Daddy always warned me about, but it had yet to bite me in the ass.

I walked away from Monroe's fresh fruit stand and walked down the rows of sellers. Some had meats and whole animals, others had vegetables; there were even some card readers and fortune tellers for anyone who came to New Orleans for that type of thing.

Those folks always made me feel a little uneasy. Not the ones in the city center, but the ones who came to the markets. They weren't flashy and they didn't hide behind doors or curtains; they were out in the open and they always looked so serious. It wasn't an act, I could tell. They firmly believed in themselves and that they had some kind of supernatural powers, so I always stayed away from them when I was a child.

I spent the next hour walking from stall to stall, looking for anything else I could purchase before I went back to Monroe's stand. He smiled when he saw me, and told his son that I was the one who had given him "so much money."

"Thank you, ma'am!" the young boy said. He couldn't have been more than ten years old, and his big, bright smile and excited brown eyes made me laugh. "Papa said we're going to eat good tonight because of you!"

"Not just tonight, good sir. You make sure that you and your papa stop by the butcher's shop in town today before you go home. Can you remember to do that for me?" I asked, crouching down to talk to him.

"Yes ma'am!" he exclaimed happily.

"Here," I said, opening my wallet and taking out a five-dollar bill. "This is for you for doing such a good job with my bag."

The young boy immediately came forward to hug me tightly. I laughed again and put a hand on the back of his head and smiled at Monroe.

"I have to go now, but I might be back

tomorrow. You have a good day now," I said as he pulled away and went back to his father to show him that he was now "rich."

They both waved at me as I walked away from their stall, bag of pineapples in one hand, and rolling luggage in the other. I needed to find a place to stay for the night, since my parents were obviously mad at me.

As I made my way back toward the street, I saw something peculiar. I saw a tall man crouched in an alley, with an animal struggling to get away from him. His face was angled down so the shadows were hiding his upper body, and I could hear him softly saying some kind of chant or whatever, before he drew a thick blade across the animal's throat and held its neck over a small bucket.

He wasn't wearing a shirt, and from what I could see, he had markings all over his arms, and I winced wondering how long they must have taken, and how painful it must've been. I figured he must be one of the locals who supplied the supernatural folk and I stopped for a brief moment to watch him curiously.

When he slowly turned his head toward me, I lowered my head and walked away as quickly as I could.

He chuckled at my gesture of what could only be considered submission and fear, and it was the last thing I heard before I disappeared around the corner from the marketplace.

He chuckled at my gesture of what could be considered submission and fear, and it was the last thing I heard before I disappeared around the corner from the marketplace.

Three

I was walking out of the butcher's shop about thirty minutes later and glanced up at the sky. The sun looked like it was going to start descending over the horizon soon, so I really needed to find a place to stay for the night. With as much as I loved this city, I knew that it could be as dangerous as it was beautiful, and I had no plans on becoming a statistic.

I was wandering down the main street in town looking for a hotel to stay in, when I came across a homeless man begging for money on the street. I watched for a moment how people walked by him like he didn't exist, until I had finally had enough and walked over to him to hand him a small wad of cash. I wasn't sure how much I gave him, but I hoped it would be enough for him to have a meal and possibly a roof over his head for a day or two.

Around the corner from where I found him was a small hotel that I hoped had a vacancy. Once Mardi Gras came along, tourists flocked here to indulge in that sin that Daddy always warned us about.

I quickly crossed the street and walked toward the heavy wooden door, pulling it open. Inside was a smoky haze and I almost left, but the threat of danger lurking out in the dark corners of the New Orleans nightlife made me walk up to the counter.

"Yeah?" the gruff old man behind the counter barked.

"Do you have any rooms?" I asked evenly. If I let on any hint of fear or self-doubt, he would catch on and charge me much more than he should. The way he looked me up and down told me that he was going to try regardless.

"I got one left. But why does a pretty girl like you wanna stay here?" he asked incredulously.

"Because I can," I replied, undoing the strap from my wrist and putting my wallet on the counter. "Now, may I please pay for the room and have a key?"

He grunted and shook his head slightly, before he pulled out a decrepit clipboard and told me to fill out my information. When I got to the first part that asked my name, I decided to use an alias. I didn't think this was the kind of place that would ask for identification, and I was paying cash anyway, so I was pretty sure it didn't matter what I put down.

Ten minutes later, I slid the clipboard back toward him and put the pen down, waiting for him to look it over and tell me how much he wanted for the room.

"Isabelle Valot?" he asked, looking up at me with curious eyes. I felt sheepish for a moment because I had used Grimm's last name, but I didn't know what else to put down.

"That's right. Now how much?" I asked, unzipping my wallet.

"I haven't seen a Valot in years," he mused to himself. I wasn't sure what he meant, but I knew that if this opened up to a line of questioning, I would crack under the pressure. I was never any good at lying.

"Your money's no good here, Miss Isabelle," he said suddenly, waving me off. "You're in room thirty seven. Here's the key. You have any trouble you come to me, Robert."

I bit my lip and looked at Robert. I was beginning to feel guilty because he was willing to give me a free room over a name that wasn't even mine.

"I wasn't born a Valot," I confessed softly. "Please tell me how much the room is."

"Who you married to then?" His curious question came out with a thicker Cajun accent than when he first spoke.

It was also that question that made me realize that in all of the years that I had spent secretly traversing the city's darkest streets and alleys with Grimm, I had no idea what his real first name was. It had never dawned on me to ask him because all I had ever known him by was what he had introduced himself to me as.

"There's only one Valot I know of that's still alive," he said, his voice becoming thoughtful. "Far as I know, he never took a wife."

"A male Valot?" I inquired excitedly.

"Yeah, it's a male. He don't have no wife that I know of," Robert said, crossing his arms over his chest, glaring at me through narrowed eyes.

He never took a wife. Maybe it's Grimm after all!

A small shock wave went through my body at the new found knowledge that Grimm had survived the hurricane's destruction.

"That goes to show how much *you* know," I quipped. "But you know what? I agree with you; a Valot's money's no good here. Give me the key and keep it quiet in this place. I need to get some rest."

With those words, I snatched the key he grudgingly held out to me, spun on my heel, and walked down the dimly lit hallway. Each room was numbered out of order, so it took me a bit to find number thirty-seven. I slid the key into the keyhole and unlocked the door. Pushing it open, I almost got knocked over by the stale smell of cigarettes and sweat. This room hadn't been aired out in a long time, and I was pretty sure I wouldn't be able to sleep very well in here. I dropped the room key and my wallet onto my bed while I debated checking out already.

I looked around the room and decided my luggage bag might be safest inside the small refrigerator in the room. I walked over to it and pulled the plug out of the wall socket behind it, before opening the door and removing the shelves. I got up and went over to the inside of the door where I had left my bag and with a sigh, brought it to the refrigerator and crammed it in. It took a few tries to get the door to stay closed, but I eventually managed it.

As I started to stand up, I lost my balance and almost fell onto the dirty carpet, barely managing to catch myself on the top of the sturdy, wooden box that had encased the fridge. I rolled my eyes; only *I* would be able to lose my balance for no reason and almost face plant onto the dirtiest carpet I had ever seen in my life.

I wiped my hands on the sides of my legs, and then went over to the bed to retrieve my wallet and the key to the room. It went without saying that there wouldn't be any food in this hotel, and I wouldn't be able to eat anything in this dingy room even if I had food delivered.

I stepped into the dimly-lit hallway and pulled the door firmly closed, locking it behind me. I was about one-hundred-and-ten percent sure that Robert wouldn't have any menus at the front desk, but he might at least be able to point me in the right direction.

The smell of incense grew heavier the closer to the front desk I got, but I welcomed the powerful scent. It was strong enough to cleanse my senses of the dirty room I had just spent maybe around ten minutes in.

When the desk was in my line of sight, I noticed that Robert was missing from his station, so I walked over and gently tapped the old golden bell that sat on the counter. I let out a sigh as I leaned an arm on it, waiting for him, or anyone really to appear.

It was right before I was about to tap the bell again that I heard the mumbled sounds of prayer. It seemed to be intensifying with each passing moment, which is probably why I hadn't heard it at first.

"Hello?" I called out gently.

I was greeted by the sound of something resembling a baton hitting the top of a drum, and then the praying stopped. Less than a minute later, Robert emerged from the back room with a tired look in his eyes.

"Yes, Miss Isabelle?" he asked, resting his hands on the counter.

"Um, I was wondering if you knew of any good places to eat around here," I replied nervously, removing my arm from the counter top.

"There's a good Cajun restaurant a few streets down. Go out onto the street and take a left out the door. Walk down a few blocks and go across the street. You'll see it just fine."

"Thank you," I replied softly as I walked quickly out of the lobby. I felt his eyes on me until I disappeared out of his range of sight, and I wondered if I should go back at all. Something about him wasn't right, and I just didn't know what it was.

Four

It was around seven o'clock the next morning when I woke up. I had decided to stuff myself full of "Louisiana's best gumbo" as it was advertised, go back to the hotel, barricade the door with the only chair in the room, and sleep in the tub. It was the one place in that room I was able to wash myself, so I knew it would be clean enough to sleep in. I didn't count on the major stiff neck I would wake up with, but it was okay with me because at least I woke up.

I didn't even bother brushing my teeth; I went to my bag, retrieved some fresh clothes, took a quick shower, and left the key on the front counter as I exited Robert's hotel.

I figured I could go back to the fresh air

market and talk to Monroe, to see if he knew of any better accommodations in town. And while I was there, I'd buy another round of pineapples for breakfast since I didn't end up eating the ones I had bought the day before. One step into that hotel room and I could only imagine what kind of bacteria had migrated to them.

I sighed as I made the trek, the humidity starting to pick up, which was a little unusual for March. I somehow managed to open my bag as I walked and pulled out a hair tie, then scooped my long brown hair back into a loose ponytail. It wouldn't do much to satiate the heat, but it would do enough for now.

As I turned toward the alley that led to the open market, I smiled when I saw Monroe's son running around the stalls. It looked like he was trying to barter with other merchants, but I was too far away to tell.

"Hey!" I called out as I neared the row of stalls. Monroe wasn't at his stall at that moment, so I assumed his son would be the one handling any business for him until he appeared. It seemed unusual to me for someone so young to be given such a responsibility, but I was sure that if he wasn't trustworthy, he wouldn't have the opportunity to trade and sell in his father's place.

The young boy was only wearing a pair of jeans with rolled cuffs; the rest of him was barefoot and shirtless. It made me wonder if it's because he was most comfortable that way, or because his family needed money more than clothes.

Careful, Emmie; you can't save everyone, my subconscious warned.

He glanced over at the sound of my voice and came running toward me with a big, happy smile on his face, and his arms opened wide. I laughed at how happy he was to see me; not in a cruel way, but in a way that told him that I was just as happy to see him.

"Hi, ma'am!" he yelled happily as he crashed against me, wrapping his thin arms around my waist.

"You can call me Emily if you'd like," I replied while returning his tight hug. "You never did tell me your name, though."

Monroe's son pulled back, arms still around me, and looked up at me with that big smile. "My name is James."

"That's a good strong name," I remarked as he pulled away. "Where's your Papa, James?"

"He's not feeling good today. Mama will be along soon, but I told them I could help until she got here," he explained.

"Is he okay?" I asked curiously.

"Ate too much steak last night," he replied with a gleam in his eye.

I smiled again. It seemed they hadn't forgotten to go by the butcher's shop after all. I was happy that I had managed to do something nice for them. I was usually a very good judge of character, and I really liked Monroe and James.

The longer we stood there just smiling at each other in silence, the more I wanted to ask him to do something for me. I would pay him for his trouble of course, but I was really hoping to ask Monroe first if it would be okay with him. Unfortunately, he wouldn't be coming to the market today from the sound of it, and I didn't really want to wait any longer than I had to.

"James, you know when I was about your age, I had a really good friend. I haven't seen him in a long time, but I think he survived Katrina because of something that was said to me yesterday," I said slowly.

"Oh, that's a dangerous place, Miss Emily. That Lower Ninth Ward? It's hard to get into and even harder to look around," he replied, shaking his head.

I sighed. At this point, if he was wary of where I was going to ask him to go, then chances were that no amount of money would change his mind. It was probably for the best.

"You think he's there?" he asked curiously.

"That's where he lived," I replied softly.

"You want me to go find him?" James prompted.

"No. Not if it's dangerous. I don't want you to be in a bad place where something could happen to you."

James shook his head firmly, "Miss Emily, you helped my Papa. You made sure we could eat for a long time; I can do this for you if you want. Tell me what he looks like."

I pursed my lips and crossed my arms over my chest. I wasn't exactly sure what he would look like now; I only remembered the boy I knew. Also, I was having serious second thoughts about James being so young and going alone to a "dangerous" place.

"What's his name, Miss Emily?" he pressed.

"I don't want you to go; not alone. And I

want to talk to your Mama first and make sure she's okay with it."

"Aw, Miss! My Mama don't need to know! I'll get some of my friends to go with me! I got older friends that always want to go out there. We'll be just fine," he declared, giving my suggestion a dismissive wave.

"I can't tell you what he looks like now; only what I remember, is that enough?" I asked softly. James nodded and crossed his arms over his chest waiting for a description and a name. "He had long, dark-blonde hair when I saw him last. Big blue eyes, skin tanned by the time he spent fishing out under the Louisiana sun. He never really smiled, but he always did with me. I think he would be about this tall now," I said, holding a hand up above my head, "and he answered to the name, Grimm. He was my very good and only friend, really."

I hadn't realized that I had been crying until James reached up to brush a tear away from my cheek. "We'll find him," he promised confidently. "As soon as Mama gets here, I'll go get my friends and we'll go find him."

I crouched down to James' height to give him a kiss on the cheek. He smiled and blushed as I stood back up and reached down for my bag. My wallet was in there and I wanted to give him some money to split with his friends. When I stood up again, I opened it up and pulled out five twenty dollar bills.

"You split this with your friends for helping me, okay?" I said, holding out the money.

"Thank you! I promise we'll do a good job of finding your very good friend," he replied happily. "Oh! There's my Mama now! I'm gonna let her know how the morning's been, and then I'll go. Don't tell her anything though, Miss Emily. If you do, she won't let me go," he warned before he ran off to greet his mother.

As I watched him chat briefly with the beautiful, dark-haired woman, I felt hopeful again.

Hopeful that he might find him.

Hopeful that he might come back with *some* news to satisfy my curiosity.

What I didn't count on was that it would be the last time I'd ever see James alive.

Five

I bought some pineapples from Monroe's wife, and she gave me some really good information about some places I could stay at that didn't reek of mold. I thanked her by giving her an extra ten dollars, then I made my way out of the market. Since Mardi Gras was tomorrow, I knew I wouldn't have a chance in hell of finding a decent place to stay, but she told me that if I went to La Rue Chateau a few streets down from Bourbon Street and told them I knew her and Monroe, they would give me a room to stay in.

It made me happy to know that she was just as kind as her husband and son. Usually families don't end up that way; there's always a good one and a bad one, but this family only seemed full of good.

My bag rumbled quietly on the cobbled path as I guided it toward Bourbon Street, which was four blocks down from the market. I could only hope that they were going to be open again tomorrow since a lot of tourists would be looking for mid-day snacks, they would be able to find plenty of fresh fruit there.

I was waiting at the intersection for the light to turn red so I could walk, when I saw a small voodoo shop on the corner. I made a note of it so that I could come back that way and see if they had any card readers or fortune tellers. I knew the ones in the market might be more authentic, but I didn't really have any important questions to ask. It would just be something to pass the time with.

When the light finally gave me the go ahead, I crossed the street and walked until I saw La Rue Chateau. It was three stories high and already decorated for tomorrow, not to mention it looked a thousand times better than Robert's moldy place.

I pushed the door open and walked up to the counter in the opulent lobby and smiled. I wasn't sure exactly how Monroe and his wife would know the people who owned a place like this, but I was definitely in a place that would make me feel safe.

There was a young, pretty, petite brunette behind the counter who smiled at me with the whitest teeth I had ever seen.

"Hello! Welcome to La Rue Chateau! Do you have a reservation?" she asked cheerfully.

"No," I replied as I approached, "But Monroe's wife sent me. She said you could find a room for me."

"Ah! Market Monroe!" she said with a big smile. "You're his friend? Then I definitely can find you a room. We're all booked up, but I always keep one vacant in case he and his family want to come watch the parade from the balcony. I'll give you their room."

I nodded happily. I was going to have a room with a balcony view of the festivities as they happened, and Daddy couldn't stop me from at least watching this time.

A few moments of tapping the keys on her computer and she had me sign some paperwork. I had no issues signing my real name in this place.

Emily I. Thibideaux, I signed with a flourish. She looked at the paperwork and nodded once she was sure all important parts were filled out.

"My name is Carrie and I'm the assistant hotel manager. Please reach out to me if you have any concerns!" she said, handing me an electronic room key. "Now you can take the stairs, or you can take the elevator up. Your room is number three-twenty. Right in the middle of the floor. Enjoy your stay!"

"Thanks Carrie!" I said, as I reached down for the handle of my bag and went toward the small elevator banks.

I already knew that once I got comfortable in the room, I was going to soak in the tub for at least an hour, and then I was going to call my parents and see if Daddy was still mad at me. I hated thinking that he would still be upset about Grimm, even after all these years. I was allowed to have friends, regardless of their position or standing in society.

The elevator came down slowly and dinged open. I stepped back to let an elderly couple pass through, and then walked in. Leaning against the mirrored back, I went up much faster than it took the mechanism to come down, and I stepped out when the elevator dinged on my floor.

Once I located my room and unlocked the door with the key card, I let out a happy sigh. The inside was just as beautiful as the outside of La Rue Chateau with a king-sized bed sitting in the middle of the room against the wall, a beautiful maple desk near the window, with a huge and comfortable looking chair sitting beside it. I took my bag over to my bed and began to take out my belongings. I wanted to utilize the balcony for airing out my clothes since they had been in the bag for so long. While that was happening, I would go soak in the tub.

I started humming a happy tune as I brought my clothes out to set them on the balcony railing. All I really had in the luggage roller was a few sundresses to prepare for the Louisiana heat, a couple of pairs of shorts, and some tank tops. Besides some bras and panties, I wasn't going to set those out on the railing, instead I let them sit on a small wooden stool chair that was sitting against the left side rail of the balcony.

As soon as that was all done, I went back into my room, leaving the balcony doors open. It would be nice to have fresh air in the room, and it might help kill the mold spores I was sure were already growing from Robert's place.

I walked back into the bedroom and pulled my clothes off. I was sure that if Carrie was as friendly as she seemed, I'd be able to give her them to have housekeeping wash.

I went toward the bathroom, the cool breeze wafting into the room and wrapping itself around my body. I pulled back the curtain and smiled. The floor of the bathtub looked immaculate, and I was satisfied that I wouldn't have to give it a scrub myself. I glanced around the bathroom until I saw a small plug sitting near the sink, grabbed it, and popped it into the drain in the tub. I turned the knobs in their appropriate directions and ran a hand underneath the water until it was a temperature I was comfortable with.

"I wish I had bubbles," I mumbled to myself.

Hm.

I saw the small bottles of complimentary hotel toiletries and grabbed the one labeled shampoo. I glanced down at the tub, then back to the small plastic bottle, before I shrugged and unscrewed the cap, letting the contents fall into the water. It wasn't what I would have hoped for, but it was enough, and it would have to do.

Reaching my hands up, I pulled my hair back into a ponytail and held it with my hands, as I went into the room to see if I could find a hair tie in my bag. *A-ha!* I thought successfully after a few moments of rummaging around in the front pockets. I held the tie in my right hand, while I reached back up again and put my hair back into a ponytail, wrapping the tie securely around it.

I wouldn't be able to wash my hair today because I had just used the shampoo as pseudo-bubbles, but I was at least going to be comfortable while I soaked in the tub.

"Just in time," I said out loud.

The water was starting to reach the middle of the tub, so I turned the knobs in the opposite direction to shut off the spout. Letting out another happy sigh, I climbed into the tub and sat down, before carefully stretching myself out. Luckily, there was a small washcloth sitting on the edge of it, so I placed it over my eyes as I laid there, letting the somewhat hot water caress my bare skin.

It was something I thoroughly enjoyed doing at home, and I always had to force myself not to fall asleep. I was afraid of drowning in the tub, so I had a small step at home that I would put at the end that I could push my feet against to keep me afloat if I ever started to slide down. Here I didn't have that, so it kept me somewhat alert as I fought the sleep that was threatening to take over me.

Lucky for me, just as I started to lose my battle, a loud eruption of laughter down on the New Orleans streets jolted me back to being completely alert.

Maybe I should've closed those damn doors after all, I thought with a sigh.

My thoughts started to drift toward Grimm. I wondered so much what he would look like now as a grown man. Would he smile if we ever saw each other again? Was he even alive to smile at anyone anymore?

God, I miss him.

Tomorrow wouldn't be a good day to try and check in with James. Even though I was sure his parents wouldn't let him go to the Mardi Gras parade, I was sure that the sudden influx of tourists would mob the streets and make it virtually impossible to move around, let alone make me want to be out in the crowd to begin with.

I would go back to see "Market Monroe" the day after and hoped that Carrie would be kind enough to let me keep the room for a few days.

I have to call Daddy and Mama when I get out of here, I thought with a yawn.

I wanted to make things right with them; I didn't want him to be mad at me because I missed my friend. Mama, I knew, wasn't mad; she just never contradicted Daddy's words.

I wasn't sure how long I had been in the tub and at what point I had actually fallen asleep, but I woke up with a start and my heart was beating erratically. I guess I had managed to tune out the people outside and lost the battle to Mr. Sandman.

Fuck, I thought, getting out of the tub and reaching down for the towel that had fallen onto the floor. I leaned down toward the drain and pulled out the plug. The water swished and made a loud gurgling sound as it disappeared into the dark hole, probably out toward the Mississippi.

I wrapped the towel firmly wrapped around my body as I went into the bedroom. It was odd that I didn't remember dreaming of anything, but it could possibly be because maybe I hadn't slept as long as it would take the body to induce dreams. With a sigh I dried myself, and let the towel fall to the beautiful carpet before I pulled back the comforter and climbed into the bed.

Perhaps a proper nap would be what I needed. I'd try to win back my parents' favor when I woke up.

Six

I was chasing James down a darkened alley, trying to catch up to him. His laughter drifted back toward me, and he called out to me.

"Keep up, Miss! I can show you where he is!"

"Wait!" I shouted out to him as my legs pumped hard, and my lungs burned. I didn't know such a young child could run so quickly and I was having a hard time keeping up.

He disappeared from view when he cut around a corner, and I found myself wavering in my movements. There was no way I'd be able to catch up to him, but he knew where Grimm was, so I had to at least try.

When I reached the end of the alley, I stopped running and looked around in confusion. I was trying desperately to catch my breath when I realized that I was standing in the Lower Ninth Ward. Did this mean that Grimm went back to his old home? Did this mean that I was going to finally see him after so many years?

"Miss! He's here!" James called out excitedly.

I took a deep breath and broke into a sprint, running blindly toward his voice. It seemed like the abandoned houses were closing in on me on either side as I ran as quickly as I could toward the laughing young boy. He had done what I had asked him to do, but why did he do it alone? I didn't see his friends anywhere, and I didn't hear any other voices besides his.

"Where are you?" I called out desperately.

"In his home! Come see what he's got in here!" James' voice rang out.

The street I ran down seemed to lengthen and I could almost swear that vertigo was setting in. I felt like the closer I got to the front door of what I assumed was Grimm's home, the further away it pulled from my reach.

A bloodcurdling scream met my ears, and it took me a moment to realize that it was James. He was in trouble and he needed my help, but why wasn't Grimm helping him?

"I'm coming!" I screamed out as the first wave of actual vertigo knocked me to my knees. I dropped onto the crooked pavement and felt my mouth begin to water. Nothing like this had ever happened to me before and I was so worried that I wouldn't be able to get to him in time.

"No! Stop please!" his voice rang out again, followed by another agonized scream.

Then silence filled the void. The only sound I could hear was that of my own heart, beating furiously in my chest as I fought to get to my feet, failing as the nausea held me

After a few moments it was over, and I was able to get to my feet. I was able to fight my way back up from the ground and I was able to run again. I barreled through the slanted wooden door and followed the dimly lit path of candles to a back room. But there was no sign of James or Grimm. Instead there was only a pool of blood in the middle of a salt circle, and some ugly deity statue at the head of it.

I woke up with a start. Never in my life had I ever dreamed of anything so insane and so blatantly violent before and my body was shaking as a result. I had no idea what the nightmare meant, but I knew that I wouldn't be going to sleep anytime soon. I didn't want to fall back into the hellish world that I had just left; it terrified me because it was a world where good children disappeared.

I sat up on the bed and pushed my sweat-dampened hair away from my forehead.

God, it was almost like I was really running, I thought leaning over the side and grabbing the towel off of the carpet. I used it to dry my face, then ran it down my arms and legs before I let it fall onto the carpet again.

Something about the air around me felt different; odd almost. As the sudden wave of paranoia washed over me, I decided to take a shower and hoped that the hot water I planned to scorch myself with,] would wash away the terrors I had just dreamt up.

Maybe coming back here wasn't such a good idea after all. As I walked into the bathroom again, I found a fresh towel in the small linen closet and turned the knobs on again. But when I stepped in and let the water start to wash over me, I wondered about James.

I knew that dreams weren't real, and I didn't believe that they held omens of any kind, but it still made me worried that maybe he had gone into the Lower Ninth Ward alone.

Stop it, Emmie, I scolded myself. *Next thing you know, you'll end up in a voodoo shop believing in the things they'll tell you about your "future."*

I chuckled at the thought. The history here was definitely rich, and voodoo played a big part in it, but I never believed in it. That was another thing Daddy had forbidden; letting us wander too far into the French Quarter alone, because if we did, we'd get "snatched up by a Witch Doctor."

These were the bedtime stories we would get. All about the big, bad, evil Witch Doctors; not once do I ever recall hearing a story about Cinderella or a princess being saved by a knight in shining armor.

I sighed as I unwrapped the small bar of hotel soap and started to lather my arms with it. Anything that would have been considered slightly normal was pretty much forbidden to do, and I think that's why I had taken such a shine to Grimm. He was far from normal and even though we didn't do much but sit around and talk while he fished, it was still the most fun I ever had as a child.

And if that's what I considered to be fun as a kid, I wonder what he's up to now. I wonder if he still sits with that fishing rod somewhere near his home. I wonder if he has a home anymore. Hell, I wonder if he's even still alive.

A sadness I had never felt before gripped me as I again considered the possibility that I might have come all the way down to New Orleans only to find out he had died. But I also knew myself well enough to know that if I hadn't come down here to at least try, I would regret it for the rest of my life.

I decided to clear my mind as I finished washing myself up. Thirty well-spent minutes in the shower had been enough to put me in a semi-decent mood again. When I was done and the water had been shut off, I dried myself thoroughly with the towel before walking stark naked out onto the balcony and leaning against the rail.

I didn't care who saw me; Daddy wasn't

around, and it was something I always wanted to do. It made me feel like Lady Godiva in a way, except I was championing for myself and no one else.

It didn't take long before one of the tourists down below whistled loudly. Now the Emmie Thibideaux that had been raised as a good girl would have immediately shied away and ran inside, but *this* Emmie Thibideaux, raised her hand and waved like she was the Queen of the Mardi Gras parade, herself.

The handsome man waved back at me before he and his friends kept walking and I felt a jolt of excitement inside of me. Maybe there was something to this whole freedom thing. Being myself instead of the little girl Daddy had raised could be fun, but I didn't want to do anything too crazy until I found out about Grimm.

I wanted to have as much fun as I could before I left New Orleans again, but I wanted to do it with *him.*

Guess I should probably call Mama and

Daddy, I thought after another ten minutes of standing on the balcony. I went back into the room and found the phone that was sitting on the stand next to the bed and dialed their number.

The phone rang and rang, but I knew eventually someone would pick up.

"Hello?" Mrs. Rourke's sweet voice asked, just as I was ready to give up.

"Hi, it's Emmie. Can I talk to Mama or Daddy?" I asked her.

"Of course you can. One moment while I find one of them," she replied sweetly.

I sighed and pulled a leg underneath my body and waited for one of them to come to the phone. I knew it would take a lot of finessing to get them to understand my point of view. But they would have to understand that they weren't the only people I loved, and while I *did* come back to New Orleans to see them, I had mostly come back to see Grimm.

With as much as I hated to think about it,

I knew it was something I would have to try to convince them to accept.

I twirled the phone cord around my finger while I waited for one of them to come to the phone, before I finally sighed and hung up. It was obvious that they were still mad at me, and it would have to be okay for now.

After the parade tomorrow, I'd go see Market Monroe and hopefully be able to talk to James. Once I found out everything he knew about Grimm, if he knew anything at all, I would swallow my pride and go to my parents' house and talk to them face to face.

But for now, I would just gather my clothes off of the balcony, dress in something comfortable, and take what I had been wearing down to Carrie and see if she'd be kind enough to have housekeeping give my used clothes a wash.

Seven

As I had previously suspected from when I first talked to Carrie, being Market Monroe's friend seemed to come with perks. She was more than willing to have my clothes and towels washed for me, and also told me that I didn't need to wait for housekeeping whenever I wanted something like that done.

I spent a couple of hours at the front desk with her just chit chatting, which was nice, since I hadn't had anyone to do that with.

In fact, I was so comfortable after about ten minutes of talking to her, that I laid out my entire reason for being in New Orleans. I told her about how upset my parents had gotten over the fact that they weren't the sole reason I had come back, and how James had vowed to help me find my friend. I didn't tell her about the nightmare though; that was too vivid still and I was trying to push it away.

"Here you go, Miss," one of the housekeepers said, coming over to hand me my perfectly folded laundry.

"Would you mind taking that up to my room, please?" I asked sheepishly. She nodded though, the pleasant smile never leaving her lips, and Carrie told her what room to go to.

"So, anyway, that's pretty much my story," I said, turning back to her with a laugh.

Carrie leaned on the counter top with a thoughtful look on her face. I wasn't sure if she had been listening or if she had tuned me out after a while, but something was definitely on her mind.

"Sorry. I must've bored you," I replied with a grin stretching across my face.

"It's not that at all, Miss Emily," she said,

her voice as thoughtful as the look on her face. "I just ... I feel like I know that person you're looking for, for some reason."

I know that should have been good news, but I couldn't help but sigh. It seemed damn near everyone I talked to so far either knew who Grimm was, or offered to help me find him, which gave me an inkling that they must've known who he was to some degree.

It's like everyone knows where he is but me, I thought in frustration.

"James won't find him though. Not if it's the man I'm thinking of. He didn't go down there alone, did he?" she inquired, turning her eyes toward me.

"Not that I know of. I mean, he promised me he would take some friends with him," I corrected myself.

"Hm."

That's it? I wanted to grab her by the shoulders and shake what information she had out of her, but I didn't want to be rude to one of Monroe's friends. Instead, I decided to try a more tactful approach.

"Seen him around, have you?" I asked, forcing the grin to stay friendly.

"Maybe once or twice. Can I give you some advice Miss Emily?" she inquired, giving me a shaky look.

"Emily is fine," I replied, holding up a hand. "And yes; advice is always welcome."

"Don't look for him anymore. Spend time with your parents if you want or go back to wherever it is that you call home now, but don't look for that man."

I raised an eyebrow at her. She pulled her arms back from the counter top and looked down at her now clasped hands. She knew something about Grimm, and she didn't want to tell me, but I had come to Louisiana for answers, and I was going to get them.

"Why not? Grimm was a decent person when he was a boy, I'm sure he's grown into a decent man," I replied defiantly.

It may have seemed silly that I was defending a man that I didn't know, but I really wasn't. I was defending the child who would let me talk his ear off for hours at a time. I was defending the child who had inspired me to compose a song and sneak him into my house so I could play it for him. *That's who I was defending.*

"I got nothing else to say," she said quietly. I watched as she began to busy herself with a thick appointment book, before she turned her back to me to place it on the counter behind her. It made me damn angry that she had bad thoughts about my friend and wouldn't tell me what they were.

"He ever come to the French Quarter?" I inquired in a loud voice.

"Sometimes."

"Carrie! What's the matter? You almost sound like you're scared of him!"

"A little bit," she confessed, her back still pointed at me.

"Why?" I asked in frustration.

She shook her head in response and almost threw herself at the front desk phone when it rang. I think she was thankful for that moment, because she knew it would stop my questions as long as she stayed on her call.

I waited as long as I could; patiently at first, but when my fingers started to involuntarily drum along the top of the counter, I knew I had to go back to my room. Listening to her constant barrage of "uh-huh" and "yes, of course" was starting to wear on my nerves.

I opened the door to the small staircase and ran up the three flights. I didn't care much for waiting for the elevator right now, I just wanted to just get out into the city, but I knew I would probably need money, and for that I needed to retrieve my wallet.

The key card unlocked the door once I slid it into the slot, and I pushed the door open in a huff. The laundry was sitting neatly on the edge of the bed and my wallet was just where I had left it; on the nightstand. I opened it up to see if I had any cash left after being everyone's personal saint by handing out money.

Should be enough, I thought, zipping it back up and walking out of the room. I let out a sigh as I took the stairs down to the main lobby where Carrie was still on her phone call. I guess she must've thought I was dumb, or maybe the person on the phone was dumb, because that was the longest phone call over vacancies I had ever witnessed.

"If you see Grimm, tell him I'm looking for him!" I called out to her as I left through the front doors.

Not that he would come to a place like this. He never did like fancy, I mused to myself as I walked down the street. I wanted to go into that old voodoo shop I had seen and get my cards read. Or maybe throw some bones; whatever they had to offer. It would pass some time and even though I had no intention of asking anything specific, chances were that whoever owned the place might have heard of Grimm too.

After all, everyone else seemed to know the man I was chasing. Even though he seemed to be little more than a ghost to me.

The Lower Ninth Ward

Eight

Most people would be ashamed to live the way I do; in an old, broken home that I had to partially rebuild, with barely enough food to last the week, and only enough water to bathe every other day if I wanted any to drink. Good thing about me is that I'm not like most people and I never gave a damn what anyone thought about me, even less so these days since I had given myself an important task to accomplish.

Keeping to myself was an easy thing. It was what I preferred, and a solitary life allowed me to do my work without prying eyes and admonishments that weren't solicited or warranted. I didn't think of myself as a bad person for what I was doing. I thought of myself as the kind of man who helped those that needed it but were afraid to ask for it.

Not once had I taken someone who would have been noticed when they went missing, until that boy came to my home. Even by his ragged clothes, I could tell he had a family who would launch a search for him, but he told me that no one knew he was here except for the person that sent him. "Miss Emily" was what he called her when I was drawing my circle. I couldn't help but think of the sweetest girl I had ever met. Her name was Emily too, if I remembered correctly, and she was the only one who had ever seen that there was more to me than my appearance.

I actually found myself feeling delighted that if it *was* her, she had sent me another saint. The boy whose name I didn't know would be number ninety-six in a long decade's worth of work, which meant I was only four more away from being done.

As I sat in my old bathtub that was missing one of its legs, leaned my head back against the cold ceramic and I thought of how the boy met his end.

It wasn't as particularly brutal as the others had been, and I was sure that I had done him a small mercy. Once my circle had been drawn, symbols put into place, and a wide enough spot for the two of us to be in without disrupting anything, I instructed him to start beating on a ceremonial drum I had. I never used it before, I just really liked it for decorative purposes, but I felt like since he was going to be the youngest saint I had made, he would most likely benefit from participating in the ritual.

Once I was sure the spirits had surrounded us and were happy with him becoming a saint, I moved quickly. I pulled him up from where he had been sitting outside the circle, drumming as if it would save his life, and used my machete to slit his throat from ear to ear. His body twitched and his hands went to his neck as I quickly picked him up and held him upside down by his ankles, letting him bleed out onto the symbols

I had drawn. I remembered closing my eyes as he gurgled, and his body began to slow down all signs of movement. While it wasn't as brutal as the path to sainthood usually was, it was crueler, and because of that, the Orishas would welcome him with open arms into the afterlife.

I stood in the circle, holding him upside down until the sun had come back up this morning. Once I was in the place that I needed to be, I could stay awake for hours if I needed to. When it was over, when the sun had broken through my busted windows, I let his ankles go and walked away after his body had made a dull thud on the wooden floor.

I had been in the tub ever since. I needed to wash away the blood and the salt before I went back to work. Spiritual currency was a big business in the underground voodoo world, and I always provided the best of everything. Bloodshed had always brought me the most income because of it being mixed with the sanctified salt.

I sighed and ran a hand back through my

hair. All the money I had hidden in this home could have bought me status and comfort, and yet I lived like a pauper. It was good for me though; it kept me grounded and on course to what I needed to achieve. Once I was done, I'd be happy and able to live my life the way I wanted. For now, I would have to accept that I had myself a servant to the whims of others and do my best to do what was asked of me.

Most people who knew of me were afraid of me. They said I took this all to a dark place, but if you want to be powerful, you have to be willing to sacrifice for it.

Closing my eyes, I draped an arm over the side of the tub and felt a smile starting to crease my lips. I was thinking about the "Miss Emily" that the boy had spoken of. I wondered if it was Emmie, and if it was, I wondered what she was doing back in New Orleans.

The last time I had seen her, she had played a song she said she had composed just for me. I remembered it clearly and would hum it to myself while I worked.

Of course, her father never cared for me. The night he chased me away before they left, he was yelling at me about being "filthy, little scum from the poor side of town" and to "stay away from his daughter."

It must've been nice to have such a big house to live in, constant food on the table, and two parents who cared enough about you to keep away the people they thought weren't worthy of being your friends.

I never really cared one way or another if he liked me or not; I hadn't gone to his house for him. I had gone to his house for his daughter, who was quite honestly the only friend I had.

I wondered about her every now and then. *Did she remember me? Did her father convince her that I was not good enough to be around her?* I liked to think she was smarter than that, but if she had come back to New Orleans and sent someone to find me, I could be wrong.

If it's even the same Emily, I told myself.

Thinking of Emmie made me think of the boy, and the work I still had to do. The only way to fully martyr him would be to cut the skin straight off of his body; no mistakes or nicks would do. I'd put his muscles in jars and make sure the bones were still intact and clean. For others like me, the bones would be the next best thing I could sell to them, because my brand of blood always sold quickly.

I opened my eyes and got out of the tub. It was time to get to work, and as today was Mardi Gras it would be a good day to find more saints, bringing me one step closer to completing my work. I would have to move quickly and quietly and hope that whoever I chose would be good enough to become a martyr.

Nine

The biggest problem I ever had in my line of work was neatly flaying the skin from a body. I lacked the patience to keep my hands steady, and as such, I'd had to discard so many victims and try again. The fact I was on number ninety six was a miracle in itself, but I hadn't gotten any better at it.

It took several deep breaths, me walking away and coming back, as well as pulling the boy's body onto my bare leg to be able to cut properly. I always did this partly naked because I didn't want to have to throw away clothes since I didn't have anything to wash the blood off with.

I let out a sigh of relief when my blade slid through the last piece of skin that was holding onto the ankle bone, and I shoved the corpse off of me. I got off of the salty, bloody floor and went to find my large mason jars. The muscles would be easy to cut off; mostly they were held together in place by thin strips of skin-like material that would always buckle under my blade with a sharp tug. If it wasn't so messy, I would actually classify it as almost fun.

But I knew that this wasn't supposed to be fun; it was a serious thing I was doing, and I was so close to being done that I could almost taste it.

When I'd found enough jars to hold his small muscles, I went back and sat down where I had left him. I started with his head, because the skull would be the most precious item made of bone I could sell if I didn't want to keep it. I turned his face to the side and put a hand gently across it as I slipped the knife underneath and began to cut away at the ends. Once I had loosened it enough, I put two fingers underneath the cheek and started to cut on the other end until I was able to pull it free. It made a wet sound when I dropped it into the jar, but I never minded it.

It took me almost two hours to completely take the muscles out and clean the bones, but when I was done, I got up, humming Emmie's song, and picked up the jars. I carried them out to one of the backrooms I hadn't quite gotten around to rebuilding yet and placed them on a small bench. I'd get around to doing something with them eventually, but for now they were of no use to me.

I used the back of my arm to wipe the sweat off of my forehead as I went back to collect the pile of skin. I gathered it all up and went into the kitchen to find bags to toss it into, before heading outside to the small pyre I had set up. No one else lived in my neighborhood at the moment, so I didn't care if anyone saw me with no clothes on.

I threw the bags onto the wooden blocks and doused it with gasoline, moving away a few feet before I lit a match and tossed it onto it.

While that was burning, I could go inside and package the bones. I figured since I was heading into the French Quarter today, I could stop by my usual buyers and see if anyone was interested. I hated going into the heart of the city, but that's where they mostly were.

I would have to find my favorite backpack to put them in. It was also the one that let my clients know that I was coming to sell and not buy.

I took a deep breath once everything was taken care of and went back to soak in the tub for a little bit. I wanted to get to Bourbon Street before noon came, otherwise it would be pure hell for me to find my next saint.

If I leave in an hour, I should be okay.

I wasn't sure what time it was because I didn't have a working clock in my home; I used the sun to gauge the different times of day and I had become quite good at it.

I really didn't want to leave until I had scrubbed everything off of my body, but it would take me a while to get there since I was going to walk for the most part. Grabbing an old t-shirt from a small pile I kept near the tub, I cleaned myself as best as I could.

Once I was done, I stepped out and walked into the small living room that doubled as my bedroom and proceeded to pull clothes out of the closet. A white button-down shirt with half sleeves, a pair of black jeans, and black slip-on shoes would have to be it for today. I wouldn't button my shirt though, because it might be hot, and I didn't want to arrive anywhere sweating.

When I was clothed, I reached around on the top of the small ledge in the closet and found my comb. I cleared my throat as I walked back into the living room and stood in front of my partially cracked mirror. I moved around in front of it a little bit until I saw enough of myself in the reflection that I was able to comb it all back, and make sure I looked neat. I glanced at my beard and sighed; I'd have to find someplace to get a trim since it was starting to look longer and wilder than I would have liked.

"It's gonna take a lot more than a comb and a trim to make you look neat and decent," I said to my reflection with a chuckle.

I leaned down and hoisted my backpack over my left shoulder before I walked out the front door. I never bothered to lock it; those few who still lived in this area knew who I was, and as such, were afraid to come near my home. I didn't bother putting out the fire in the backyard either. If the house burned down it would be a vast improvement to what it was now, but I also knew that the spirits protected me, so I wouldn't have to worry about it.

With a deep sigh, I started the long trek to the French Quarter, hoping that I would make some good sales today.

Mardi Gras

Ten

It took less than the hour I had been hoping for by the time I got to Bourbon Street. The first place I was going to stop was Marie's Cove of Voodoo, because not only did she have the most money of all my buyers, she was always looking to be supplied.

I walked past the La Rue Chateau hotel and rolled my eyes when I almost got run over by a small group of college-aged girls who were laughing loudly and talking about how drunk they planned to get.

None of them would make good saints; they would be missed by someone, and I didn't like to use foolish people either—it tainted the magic.

I went down a few blocks then crossed the street, and as I pushed the door open, a small young woman walked out in a huff, flipping her dark hair over her shoulders.

"Ah! Grimm Valot!" Marie's old, powerful voice rang out.

"Didn't like what you told her?" I asked with a laugh, as I walked over and let her wrap her arms around me.

Priestess Marie was a small, stout woman who had immigrated from Barbados. She had white hair that she kept under a white wrap, and always wore a dress of some kind. Her face was lined with age and wisdom, but her narrow brown eyes were as young as the day was long.

"That girl doesn't matter right now, but I want to talk to you about her," she replied, her eyes filling with mystery.

I nodded and handed her my backpack. She waved at me to follow her into her back room where she would hold her ceremonies that were worth more money than any person could usually afford, but desperation ran rampant in the world, and she could profit from it greatly.

Leaning against the wall inside the curtain, I waited patiently while she pulled out the young boy's bones and the bowls of blood.

"How old was he?" she asked, examining the bowl.

"Couldn't have been more than ten," I replied thoughtfully.

"Oh, he's a saint now!" she cackled. "I'll take it all. Come back to the front, I got money for you there."

She handed me my empty backpack as she went by me. I wasn't sure how old she was, but she moved faster than most people that I assumed were around her age would be able to. I went around the front counter and waited while she leaned down and pulled out two thick, brown, paper bags and handed them to me.

"Thank you," I said, taking them from her. "Now, you said you wanted to talk to me about that girl?"

A slow smile spread across her face as she pulled herself up onto the white wooden stool that sat behind the counter. I used the time to put the paper bags into the backpack, before slinging it over my shoulder again.

"That girl was looking for you," she hissed through her smile.

"For me?" I asked curiously.

"She said she was looking for Grimm; you're the only Grimm I know."

I turned around and walked to the front door and pulled it open, but she was nowhere to be found. Was this the same person who had sent the last saint to me?

"Did she say why?" I asked from the door.

"She did, but I want something from you

before I tell you," Marie said, her voice dropping to a low, powerful tone.

I let the door close and walked back to the counter, curious as to what else I could possibly give her.

"I want a promise," she said, when I placed my hands on the counter.

"What kind of promise, Marie?" I prodded.

"I want you to promise me that when you and that girl find each other, you will bring me her blood. She's a good girl, Grimm. I saw it when I read her cards. You *will* find each other again and that's the price for the information I will give you."

I let my head fall back and I let out a sigh. Obviously, Marie had found another saint for me, and even though I should have been grateful, I found myself feeling like I was being set up. She may have been good to me all these years by purchasing my wares, but I knew that getting into business with her could lead to trouble. It didn't matter though; four more saints and I would be untouchable.

"Alright," I finally said, looking back down at her.

"You give me your hand first, Grimm Valot. I want to see if you're lying to me," she commanded sternly as she held her own hand out.

I shook my head and chuckled, but I dropped my hand–palm up–into hers and waited while she squinted and looked. Marie had tried this before; to read the lines on my hands and see if I was lying to her or not, and every time she had tried it, she was unsuccessful, so I wasn't worried.

"Damn," she finally said, letting my hand go and shaking her head. "I still can't see nothing."

"I gave you my word, Marie. Now give me the information you have," I replied in an even tone.

"Her name is Emily Thibideaux. She's

staying just down the street at La Rue Chateau. I saw the card when she opened her wallet. But be careful Grimm; even the smallest creature can lead to the downfall of a powerful man like you," she warned with a smirk on her face.

It is *Emmie,* I thought in a stunned silence. I knew the look on my face gave way to the shock I was feeling because Marie slammed her fist on top of the counter angrily.

"You remember your promise to me, Grimm Valot, or *no* spirit will be able to keep you safe from me."

"Yeah," I replied, not really listening to her. "You have my word."

I turned around and walked out of Marie's Cove without a care in the world about her threat. She should've known better than to take the word of a killer to heart, but if I wanted to keep her as a buyer, I would have to bring Emily's blood.

I'd have to find Emmie, and I'd have to do it before Marie sent her dogs out to get the blood for her.

Fuck, I thought irritably, as I started to make my way to La Rue Chateau. I only hoped that she would've gone back to the hotel instead of out into the crowd. Her life was depending on it.

Eleven

I stopped a few doors down from La Rue Chateau and mulled over my options. If I was going to make Emmie a saint, surely, I would give her the privilege of being the last one. But if I was going to do my best to get her the hell out of New Orleans, would it be worth living the rest of the time looking over my shoulder before I had a chance to complete my work?

And who exactly would I be saving, anyway? I wasn't sure if she was still *my* Emmie, or if she was someone completely different now. The only way that I would be able to find out for sure was to walk into the hotel and ask for her.

I ran a hand back through my hair to

make sure it was still presentable as I made my way to La Rue Château. When I pulled the doors open and walked in, I saw someone quite familiar. The girl behind the counter had come so close to being a saint once, but when I realized that she wanted my body instead of being a part of a greater plan, I let her go before my intentions became clear.

I had to keep my body and soul pure to be able to complete my work, because becoming tainted would corrupt it all.

I smiled as I approached the counter, hoping that she would remember me well enough to know not to lie to me, but *not* remember me well enough to assume I wasn't still a threat. Even if I couldn't martyr her, I could still sell her bones for a handsome fee if she tried to cause trouble for me.

She looked up from her papers with a smile at first, but when our eyes met, the blood left her face. The only other time I had ever seen that was when I was the permanent cause of it, and I couldn't help but be fascinated in this moment.

"I ... Um ... Welcome to ..." her voice faltered off and I had to bite back my laughter. It appeared that she had remembered me after all.

"I'm not here for you," I said, putting my backpack on the floor. "I'm here for someone else."

"Okay," she replied uneasily.

"Emily Thibideaux is staying here, yes?" I asked, leaning an arm on top of the counter.

She nodded but didn't say much else. She didn't move to get me any information either, which is what I had been expecting; a name in exchange for the information.

"Did she come back? Is she in the hotel right now?" I asked irritably.

"I'm sorry, but I can't give out any information on our guests," she replied softly.

I stared at her for a moment, trying to decide how to proceed. Should I take her, destroy the tapes, and drain her of blood, or try to smile and start all over again?

The boy did *say Emmie was looking for me.*

"She's expecting me," I said.

"Your name?" she asked, picking up the multi-line phone on the desk behind the counter.

"Just tell her I'm an old friend, "I replied evenly.

The girl with the beautiful, long brown hair nodded and turned her back to me as she punched the room number into the phone and waited.

"Miss Emily?" she finally said softly. "You have a visitor. He said to tell you he's an old friend."

I waited patiently while she listened for a moment, before she slowly nodded her head, and hung up the phone.

"She'll be down shortly. You can wait over there," she said nodding at a square formation of leather chairs in the lobby.

I let out a small sigh as I leaned down to pick up my backpack and headed to the chairs. I decided to sit on one that would give me a full view of the lobby. This way I could see Emmie when she appeared and decide what I wanted to do with her. Even though I didn't fear Marie, I also didn't want to lose the business.

I crossed one leg over the other and waited patiently. When I heard the distant ding of the elevator, for some reason, I felt myself becoming nervous and I cleared my throat quietly, training my eyes on the hallway that led straight to the front desk.

It felt like a lifetime before I saw the small woman who had almost knocked me over leaving Marie's shop walk up to the counter and talk to the girl who could have become one of my saints. After a few moments of conversation, the would-be saint nodded in my direction, and Emmie spun around.

I smiled and stood up. The look on her face went from curiosity to understanding in a matter of moments as she practically ran over to where I was sitting.

"Grimm?" she asked excitedly as she neared me.

"Emily Thibideaux," I replied, the smile still on my face.

"Oh my God! Grimm!" she shrieked, reaching up to wrap her arms around my neck.

I would be lying if I didn't say that it made me feel uncomfortable, but I let her have her moment of joy without putting up a fight. Instead, I put my arms briefly around her waist, then gently pulled her back and looked into her pretty brown eyes.

"It's been a long time," I said softly.

"I can't believe it!" she exclaimed, her face lit up like the Louisiana skyline we used to watch. "I've been looking for you for days! Oh, I'm so glad you're okay!"

She reached up to hug me again, but I grabbed her by the wrists and pulled her down into the seat next to me. She didn't seem to mind as she sat down and placed her hands between her legs.

"I'm trying not to cry right now," she admitted, with a laugh.

"Why would you cry?" I asked curiously.

"Years of not knowing if my best friend was alive or dead, silly," she replied, using the tips of her fingers to wipe under her eyes. She really *was* fighting tears, and I felt the smile on my face widen slightly.

"You don't look a thing like I remember," she said shyly. "You're all grown up now."

"It tends to happen as the years pass. You still have the same girlish face you did when we were kids, though," I remarked thoughtfully.

"So, how have you been?" she asked, putting a hand on my leg.

I looked down for a moment, then quickly pulled my leg up underneath myself, forcing her to move her hand. I hated being like this with Emily, but I didn't want to feel anything I shouldn't, and because of that, I would do my best to keep myself untouched in any and every way.

"Good. How about you?" I asked, clasping my hands behind my head.

"I've been okay. I moved away before Katrina. I mean, you obviously knew that, but when Mama and Daddy came back, I kinda made a break for it. They would come and visit me and stuff, but I finally got to the point where I missed New Orleans so much that I knew I had to come back. Besides, I would have these weird dreams where we'd be sitting over at Old Algiers and a tidal wave would come and take you away. It gave me a lot of sleepless nights, so I knew I had to look for you when I came back," she said softly.

There was no way I would be able to martyr her. She was the perfect candidate for it; selfless, kind, and I couldn't smell the stench of the men that had been inside of her–if any at all–but she cared too much about me still and it would haunt me even after everything was said and done.

"Where do you live these days? I'd love to see your place before I leave," she said brightly.

It was an honest attempt to change the subject because it made her sad, but that was the last thing I wanted to have happen. Emily in my home wouldn't be a good idea, because no matter how much I could fight it now, I wouldn't be able to fight the call there. Not now, when I was so close to being done.

"Same place," I replied quietly.

"Wait, I thought that the Lower Ninth Ward was abandoned," she said in confusion.

"Not all of it. Next time you come to New Orleans, I promise to take you," I said, thinking quickly. By that time, I would be done, and she wouldn't be in any danger. "But I think you should spend time with your family while you're here."

"Grimm Valot, you wait one minute," she said evenly. "I've seen my parents, I've even seen the help, but this is the first time I'm seeing *you* in years, and you can't get rid of me that easily."

The smile left my face. I didn't like being argued with, and Emily was no exception to that rule, regardless of friendship or not.

"Listen, I have to do some stuff at home, and I need to get out of here before Mardi Gras starts. Are you staying here long?" I asked.

"Few more days," she replied unhappily.

"I'll come back for you tomorrow," I promised, getting to my feet.

"Why can't you just stay and go home tomorrow? I've got this big, huge bed all to myself and we can watch the parade from my balcony," she suggested, getting to her feet.

I sighed and ran a hand back through my

hair. It almost pained me that she didn't know what kind of person I had turned into. If she did then she wouldn't have bothered to look for me, and I wouldn't be standing here trying not to hurt her feelings.

"Tomorrow, Emmie," I replied, shaking my head. "I'll come back tomorrow."

She crossed her arms over her chest and glared at me. "This better be the most important thing in the world you're doing. And if you break your promise and don't come back tomorrow, I'll go to the Ward and find you."

I chuckled. Emmie had always been a fierce little thing. The day her father chased me out of their house, I remember her trying to grab onto him and stop him, but she was just too small at the time.

I looked down into her eyes for a moment. I always liked her eyes because they were so warm and friendly. She really was the only person who ever cared about me, and I needed to find a way to get her to see what I had become without hurting her in the process.

"You have my word; I'll come back for you tomorrow morning," I replied softly.

A satisfied smile spread across her pretty face as she reached up yet again to hug me, this time kissing me on the cheek. I closed my eyes for a moment before I opened them again and smiled back at her.

Then I walked out of La Rue Chateau to find what I knew I needed. Three more saints would be made tonight, because I wouldn't have the time to do it tomorrow.

After all, I had given Emmie my word that I would be back for her. I just didn't know in what sense I meant it, and I would have to get to work tonight to keep her safe tomorrow.

Twelve

I left the French Quarter and went over to Old Algiers. I wanted to sit on the grass and think for a while about what I was going to do. I knew I would have to go back when the celebrations were in full swing and take whoever I could find. With as much as I didn't want to be reckless about my choices, whoever was unaware of the danger in coming close to me would be the one I would take. I needed to take at least three, and I wondered how the hell I was going to manage that.

The closer I get to being done, the safer she'll be from me, I thought as I looked out over the Mississippi River.

A part of me wanted desperately to save

her from what I knew should happen to her. Marie's shop wasn't far from where Emmie was staying and I would have had to find a way to keep a watch on her from my home, but I had no idea how to do it.

The other part of me knew that Emmie's life source—her blood and bones—would make me so much money that I would probably never have to steal the innocent and sell their pieces and fluids for a generous sum.

Does she have to die? How do I save her from her when I don't know if I can really save her from myself?

I sighed and leaned back onto the palms of my hands. The breeze that went by made me smile slightly as I watched the water ripple lazily. I couldn't think about Emmie's salvation when all I had on my mind was destruction. The world didn't work that way, because if it did, there would be no one left to wage wars or try to make peace.

Who do I take? I wondered tiredly, placing my face in my hands. I was so close to being done but I was also tired too. The remorse after ninety-six saints still hadn't set in, so I knew that four more would affect me even less.

Was I a monster for what I believed in, or was I just a man who knew that everyone has to die at some point, and sending them off on a greater purpose was the best thing for them?

In their last few breaths, they had all seen me as the devil in disguise. I was waiting for the one who would see me as their savior, understanding that I had done something great for them—as well as for myself.

Behind me in the distance somewhere, I could hear the sounds of children laughing, and I knew I would have to get to work. First, I wanted to go to the market and see if it was open. The purpose was to shake the hand of the man whose son had become my most recent saint and give him the money that Marie had paid me for his bones and blood. I wouldn't tell him who I was or why I was giving him the money, but it was my custom to pay the families–if I could find them–for the use of their loved ones.

Would it ever be enough to halt their mourning? No, but that wasn't the point of it. It was to give them some kind of comfort and reparation for their sacrifice.

I got to my feet and slung my backpack over my shoulder. When I turned around, I almost slammed into Emmie, who I didn't even know had been standing behind me.

"Brings back memories, doesn't it?" she asked softly.

"I told you to stay put," I replied, harsher than I meant to. My tone didn't seem to bother her, instead she just walked past me and leaned against one of the trees while looking at the river.

"I know," she said with a loud sigh. Emmie turned, giving me a sidelong glance. "I just don't believe you when you say you'll come back for me tomorrow."

"Emmie, go back to the hotel. I told you I

would come for you tomorrow, and I will."

She held my gaze to see if I would break it first or look away because that would mean I was lying. What she didn't understand was that the life I started to live after she left, enabled me to put on such a spectacular façade that no one would ever know when I was telling the truth unless I showed them.

"Eight sharp, Grimm. Otherwise I'm coming to find you," she finally said, holding up a warning finger.

"Eight sharp," I confirmed. "Come on; let me walk you back to the hotel."

She glanced out at the Mississippi River one more time before she nodded and fell into step beside me. From the direction we were coming in, we would have to pass Marie's shop and I knew she would see us if she wasn't busy doing a reading. I could only hope she did; I would give her a nod as a false confirmation of her request, but also let her see me with Emily. It would be a sure way to keep her and her dogs at bay and give me a chance to either get her out of this damn place or keep her inside of me forever.

I let her chatter away the entire way back to La Rue Chateau. I responded every now and then with a sound of agreement or surprise of some sort to let her know that I was interested in what she was saying. When the moment came to walk past Marie's Cove of Voodoo, I made sure to keep Emily on the side furthest away from the door; especially when I saw that Marie was standing outside talking to a would-be-patron.

"Ah, there he is now!" she exclaimed loudly.

Emily started to slow her pace so we could stop and talk to Marie, but I put a hand on her elbow, shot the voodoo priestess a dirty look, and crossed the street with her immediately. A few cars honked angrily at us, but I didn't care. If Marie was pointing me out to someone, it was for spiritual purposes and that was a part of me Emily didn't need to see or know about just yet.

"You know that crazy old lady?" Emmie asked me curiously, as we weaved past a couple of parked cars and onto the sidewalk.

"Sort of," I replied through gritted teeth as I let go of her elbow. "Just keep walking, we're almost there."

"Ugh. She's crazy with a capital C," Emmie said, shaking her head. "Don't think I'm weird for this, but I went to her and had her do a reading for me and she told me the most bizarre stuff that had nothing to do with what I asked."

"Like what?" I asked, glancing down at her.

"She just went on and on about saints and blood and bones, and how I was so much prettier on the inside than I was on the outside. It's like I paid her all that money for absolutely nothing," she said, throwing her hands in the air.

I swallowed hard. I felt like my throat was swelling up, which meant that I would most likely work against my own will. Marie's readings were never wrong, and I knew I wouldn't have a choice now. When we reached the doors to La Rue Chateau, I looked down at Emily Thibideaux with sadness tearing my heart into pieces.

"I love you, Emmie," I said softly.

"I love you too, Grimm," she replied with a big smile. "It's good to know that we're still friends like this, you know."

"Get out of New Orleans tonight and don't come back," I commanded, gently giving her a push toward the doors, before I turned around and tore down the street.

I refused to make her a martyr.

I refused to make her a saint.

After tonight, after the next three, I would find someone else who was just as appealing to Marie as Emmie was, and then it would all be over.

But I refused to take her life, no matter

what the cost would be.

Thirteen

I had fought the demons for longer than I could remember. I can't exactly say I was chosen, but I can't say that I would have declined if I had been. I always wanted to see what humans were really made of, ever since we had lost so many when the rains came, but what I wanted most of all, was knowing that nothing would ever be able to hurt me again.

The day I decided to embrace the demons was the day I became what I am. I chose to start selling the bones and blood shortly after I met Marie. She told me she could see what I did when she closed her eyes at night, and she told me that if I kept her well stocked, she would keep my discretions in the dark, as well as compensate me for what I could bring to her.

But as I made my way back toward Bourbon Street, I found myself feeling the demons swell from within. Not the mythological demons of old, but my own, personal demons that clawed at my soul and had led me down this path of darkness and destruction.

I need to finish this. I need this to be over so I can live whatever life is in store for me afterward.

As I wandered down toward the crowds that were already starting to gather, I found myself looking for Emmie. I needed her to stay out of sight, especially now that the crowds were gathering. If she came out into the streets, Marie would be able to have her taken without anyone knowing.

Focus. You're here for saints, not Emily Thibideaux.

The bustling and excitement around me

was causing me to sweat. I had a problem being around crowds, because I was best known for being more of a myth. Not many people knew who I was by looking at me, and I wanted to keep it that way.

I grunted as a group of young men who were already drunk pushed past me on their way to their next bar. If I had my machete on me, I would have probably flown into a frenzy and gutted them for touching me.

Times like this were when I had to remind myself that I wasn't a murderer. I was a man of sacrificial purposes; murderers were evil people who killed for the thrill of it.

I sighed unhappily as I scanned the crowd. Almost everyone around me was tainted in one way or another, which meant that if I couldn't find people like Emmie, I'd have to purify them with fire. That always made the process of cleaning the bones messy, and I would usually lose out on money I could get for them if I let them stay in the pyre for too long.

Then it happened.

The same group of young women who had pushed past me on my way into La Rue Chateau were walking toward me, one of them with long, blonde hair was smiling at me through a drunken haze.

"You're hot!" she called out as they approached.

It took everything I had not to raise my hand to cover my nose. The smell of alcohol on her was so strong, I was surprised she could still stand.

"What's your name?" she asked, stopping in front of me.

"Kemper," I replied, with a forced smile. I hated smiling unless it was with Emmie, since she was the first and only one who ever received a true, genuine one from me.

"I'm Larissa," she said with a big smile. I fought the urge to roll my eyes when she hiccupped and giggled. "Sorry."

By count, there were five of them, so I would have to separate the three most inhibited from the other two and convince them to come back to the Lower Ninth Ward with me.

"Here for the parade?" I asked, crossing my arms over my chest. The backpack slid a little bit down my arm, so I hoisted it back up quickly. *Fuck, I forgot to go to the market.*

"Yeah. We're here to find a sexy local man too, and I think we found him, didn't we girls?" she asked, lust taking hazing over her drunken eyes.

Please don't touch me.

"Know anyone interested in a good time?" she purred, stepping closer. My instinct told me to take a step back, but I needed her and two of her friends.

"I might."

"Where are you staying?" she asked.

Is this really going to be so easy?

"I don't live around here. But I can take you back to my place if you'd like to see what New Orleans really looks like," I replied coyly.

"I'm game," she replied happily. "You girls wanna see where Kemper lives?" she asked her friends.

One of her friends, who wasn't as intoxicated as the rest of them, was eyeing me warily. I let my eyes meet hers and she ended up looking away.

"I'm gonna go finish the bar crawl," she said quietly.

No you're not, I thought evenly.

"Come on, it'll be fun. I promise I'm harmless and I'll have you back in time for the parade. Besides, Larissa wants to have a good time," I said, nodding at her. She was wavering on her feet at this point, and I wondered how much longer I had before she would either pass out or change her mind.

"Tell you what," I said, as she looked me up and down again, "I've got some moonshine at home that I just dug up a few days ago. You girls can come over and drink while I give Larissa what she obviously came for, and then I'll bring you all back."

"I don't know," she said cautiously.

"You girls into magic, by any chance?" I asked suddenly.

"Like voodoo?" she asked, her eyes becoming wide.

"How about I show you what an authentic ceremony looks like after I'm done with Larissa? It'll be ... educational. And free."

The four of Larissa's friends put their heads together. They were obviously concocting a plan in case something went wrong, but this wouldn't be the first time that I had dealt with more than one martyr.

"Deal," she finally agreed, once they broke out of their huddle.

"What's your name?" I asked her, the smile on my face widening slightly.

"Reagan," she replied, holding out her hand.

I took her hand against my better judgment and shook it firmly. I had to gain her trust though, and I knew it was the cordial thing to do. Not taking her hand would have sent up more red flags than she was already fielding, and I couldn't have that.

"It's nice to meet you girls," I said, when we let each other go. "Follow me; it's a bit of a walk, but I guarantee it'll be worth it."

And Reagan will go into the fire first.

Fourteen

Emmie

Grimm didn't know, but I had been watching him from the balcony outside my room. He was easy to spot in the growing crowd of people, because of the way his white shirt hung open, the tattoos that lined his arms, and how he trudged unhappily along. Nothing of what he had been doing bothered me until I saw him stop to talk to that group of drunken college girls. What really hurt my feelings was when I saw them walk out of sight with him, when he couldn't find time for his childhood best friend.

I did what any normal, concerned friend

would do. I followed them away from the French Quarter, past the Old Algiers, and into a part of New Orleans that he had always forbidden me from going to.

But today was going to be different. I was going to follow them and see what it was that he was trying to hide from me. I liked to believe he wouldn't touch those girls; not in *that* way, but I only knew the boy version of him and still had to learn about the man he had turned into. I couldn't help but think that he was hiding something from me. Little things like steering me away from the crazy lady who owned the voodoo shop, and telling me to leave Louisiana, just threw up red flags all over the place for me.

Should I have cared that everything inside of me was screaming at me to leave it alone? I would imagine so; but I didn't come this far to see him, get chastised for it, and then shooed home.

Daddy was mad at me for wanting to see Grimm. Mama wouldn't stand up for me, hell she wouldn't even stand up for herself.

Grimm seemed more interested to see me than happy, and it was really messing with my head. I figured if I followed him and saw what it was that he was up to, maybe we could find a way to connect on some level, and we could do it together before I left.

I went into the bedroom after I made a note of which direction they were headed in and pulled on my running shoes. I wasn't much for running, but I was very capable of sprinting long distances if I needed to.

I took the stairs down and waved at Carrie as I walked quickly past the front desk. I wasn't sure if she waved back or even saw me, but I knew it was the cordial thing to do. Once I was out on the sidewalk, I walked around to the side of the hotel my room was on and looked up.

Okay, so if he was heading that way when I was up there, then that's where I need to go.

Taking a deep breath, I broke into a fast-paced jog. It wasn't exactly running, and it wasn't exactly sprinting, but it was just fast enough to allow me to catch up to Grimm and his new friends before I lost them completely.

I wasn't exactly sure where I was going, but I hoped that the streets would eventually intersect at some point. Something told me to go toward the Old Algiers spot that he and I loved as kids, and I could only hope he wasn't there with them. It would taint our special place, even if it wasn't just ours anymore.

Come on, Grimm. Which way did you go? I wondered desperately to myself after ten minutes of blindly chasing him with no promise of catching him in sight.

I took a left turn and decided to turn my jog into a sprint. I wanted to know if he was where my heart was telling me he might be, but once I got to our place, I saw that I was wrong. He wasn't there and he hadn't been there recently. I knew it because I couldn't catch his scent on the air; Grimm had a very peculiar smell to him. Almost like myrrh mixed with patchouli, and it was strong enough to linger if he stayed in one place long enough.

The only place left to go is the Lower Ninth Ward. He'll be so angry at me for it, but I don't care.

It was when that decision engraved itself into my mind that I realized I had no idea how to get there. Maybe if I was lucky, Monroe, his wife, or James would be in the market, and I could ask one of them.

Fifteen

When I reached the small alley that opened into the market, I slowed my pace and began to take deep breaths. It was a trick I had taught myself to reinstate my regular breathing quicker than normal, and I didn't want to end up at my favorite pineapple stall doing some heavy breathing. I couldn't explain it, but it would just seem rude to me.

I took one last deep breath and tied my hair back into a loose ponytail as I let it out. I was sure that the wind had done wondrous things to my hair, and I didn't want to scare whoever was manning the stall today by being out of breath and crazy-haired.

Once I was sure I was somewhat presentable, I stepped out of the edge of the alley that seemed to always be encased in darkness, and into the bustling, sunny market area.

"Oh," I mumbled in disappointment. Monroe's stall was closed up, but there was someone standing near it that I didn't know. The man was tall and bone thin; somber would be the best way to describe the look on his face.

Our eyes locked for a moment, which prompted a nod from him. I bit my lip nervously, but I approached him anyway. I liked Monroe, and something told me that the happy man who was known fondly as Market Monroe must have serious things to take care of if his stall was closed.

"Hi," I said softly when I reached the man. Being close to him kind of scared me. The whites of his eyes were almost completely sickly yellow in color, and he was missing a couple of teeth. His brown skin must have been pretty and flawless once, but you'd never know it underneath the layers of scars that were visible because of his rolled up sleeves and denim shorts.

"Looking for Monroe?" he asked in a dry voice.

I nodded, clasping my hands in front of me. I had a feeling this man wouldn't hurt me, so I was starting to relax a bit.

"He's not here."

"I can see that," I replied carefully. "Is he coming today? I need to ask him something."

"He won't be back for a long time. His son's missing. He's out looking for him. I doubt he'll ever find him, though," he said, shaking his head.

I raised an eyebrow. Come to think of it, I hadn't seen or heard from James since I had sent him to find Grimm. But Grimm didn't make mention of seeing the boy, did he? I couldn't remember.

It's probably not James anyway; he's not the only son they have, I'm sure.

"Which son is it?" I asked, clearing my

throat.

"How do *you* know him?" he inquired evenly. His sickly eyes narrowed as he crossed his bony arms across his chest. I got a better view of the scars; deep, ragged, and almost white. *It almost looks like he had fought off a monster and won.*

"I buy pineapples from him. He's my friend," I replied, tearing my eyes away from his scars and forcing myself to look him in the eyes.

"Then why did you ask which son?" he scoffed. I noticed that the more agitated he got, the heavier his accent became.

"I just wanted to be sure it was James," I said softly and lowering my eyes.

And if it really was James, then I was responsible for finding him, not his father. I looked up at the man who was giving me an odd look. I figured if anyone knew where I needed to be, it would be him.

"How do you get to the Lower Ninth

Ward?" I asked.

"That's no place for a princess like you," he said, shaking his head firmly. The word 'princess', though not implied in a condescending way, brought a fire out of me. I was angry that my appearance always meant I should assume myself to be better than everyone else, and it just wasn't true.

I had no choice but to give up chasing Grimm now. James was missing and I was pretty sure that he had at least made it into the Lower Ninth Ward. If I ran into Grimm there, he'd have to get over it. Besides, he had company to keep his attention; I had a possibly scared little boy to save.

The Bad Man

Sixteen

I wasn't exactly scared, but I wasn't sure of myself either. If James was in a dangerous situation, how would I be able to get him out of it? I didn't have any money on me, and I was pretty sure that smiling and batting my eyelashes wouldn't get him out of it.

Fuck. I really should have come up with a plan on the way over here.

It wasn't as bad as I thought it would be, and I knew I was here by the drastic scenery change. There were still broken homes, things strewn about, and there was a more desolate feeling on this side of New Orleans, but it wasn't the ghost town I was expecting. Some houses had small, started gardens in front, and others had pleasant little figures on their lawns.

It was obvious that the rebuilding would take more time, but I thought they were making excellent progress and I found myself wondering if I could get Daddy to lend some money to the cause.

Daddy's a good man. He'll do it if he comes to see what they're really going through, I reasoned to myself.

And that was my plan as I saw it. Find James, then go back to my parents' house, and convince Daddy to come back with me somehow.

A small group of children on old bicycles were riding toward me, laughing and shouting at each other. I walked into the middle of the street, hoping they would see me instead of running me over, and at the last second, the oldest of the group did.

"Be careful!" he shouted at me.

"Wait, I wanna talk to you," I said firmly, stepping in front of his now stopped bicycle and placing my hands on the handlebars.

"We don't got no time for rich girls," one of the younger boys said dismissively.

"You do today," I snapped at him. "I'm looking for someone; two people really, and I want to know if you've seen either of them."

"You got names?" the older boy asked.

I nodded, "James is the first one. His father runs a fresh fruit stall in that little market over in the city. He … he came this way because I asked him to help me find a friend of mine, but he never went home."

The group of children looked at each other silently. It was obvious they knew something, but no one seemed willing to talk.

"I'll take you into the city and buy you all new bikes, if you help me out," I said, crossing my arms over my chest.

Almost immediately they all broke into friendly smiles. They knew that a "rich girl" like me would be able to make good on that promise. But I noticed that the oldest boy had a bothered look on his face.

"James, you said? I ran into a boy with that name a couple of days ago," he admitted quietly. "But, Miss, I don't think you gonna like what you find."

"He was the one who was looking for the bad man, wasn't he?" the youngest boy asked thoughtfully.

"Who's the bad man?" I asked him wearily.

The oldest boy hopped off of his bicycle, set it on the kickstand, and took me by the hand. I let him lead me slowly down the street until we reached an intersection where he stopped.

"Go all the way down that street until you feel the fear. You *will* feel it the closer you get, Miss. That's where the bad man is. That's where James went even though I told him not to go there," he said shakily.

"What's your name?" I asked, putting an

arm around his thin shoulders. I did it for no other reason than to calm him down, but I was worried that from the way he was shaking, it would take more than that to make him feel safe again.

"Jeffrey," he replied quietly.

"Jeffrey, can you please tell me who the bad man is?" I asked, giving him a squeeze.

His lower lip trembled, and he kept his eyes on the end of the street he had been directing me down. To my surprise, he used the back of his hand to wipe tears away, and then he looked up at me.

"I don't know his real name. I told James not to go, but he said he made a promise he wanted to do his best to keep. I tried to stop him; I swear it. I told him all about the bad man, but he didn't care," he said, a sob escaping him.

I hugged him close to me, letting him cry into my chest. I felt terrible for having made him cry, but I wanted to know who the bad man was. In my heart, I had a feeling I knew who he was talking about, but I wanted desperately to be wrong.

I was beginning to feel like it was useless. There was no way he would stop crying long enough to tell me what I already knew in my heart; what I refused to believe.

The rest of the children came over to surround us. The youngest one was looking at me as though he was debating to tell me what Jeffrey couldn't.

"Did he tell you yet?" he asked curiously.

"No," I replied quietly.

"He's scared of him. We all are, so we stay far away. He does voodoo, but he does it all wrong. He kills people is what we hear, kills them dead and tears them up to sell their pieces to that voodoo queen Marie and whoever else does it wrong too. You should stay far away from him. If that boy didn't come back, it's 'cause he can't," he warned, holding up a finger.

I let go of Jeffrey and looked down the desolate street that was supposed to make me feel the fear of getting closer to the bad man; the one who killed people and sold them on some kind of black market for voodoo. I don't think I had ever felt as angry as I did at that moment. They had to be wrong, because if they weren't then I didn't know what I was going to do.

"What's the bad man's name?" I asked for what felt like the millionth time.

"The name he goes by is Grimm," the young boy said. He reached over and grabbed Jeffrey by the arm as they all ran back toward their bikes, leaving me standing there.

At the beginning of the empty street of fear where I would find the bad man; as a child he had been my best friend in the entire world, and as a man he had become a monster.

Seventeen

Grimm

The amount of nonsense that was being talked and giggled about as we walked toward my home was enough to make me want to scream. It also solidified that I was doing the right thing by keeping to myself until I had wares to sell, and living in a part of the Ward that I knew people wouldn't come to unless they were looking to become part of my inventory.

I wasn't exactly sure how I was going to subdue all five of them, but I only needed three to be part of the ritual. If I wanted to, I could make it easy on myself, kill one, martyr the remaining four and be done, but I still wasn't sure which ones would be purified and worthy until the flames consumed them.

I could see my house from where we were, and I hoped they would go in willingly. If they didn't, it wouldn't be a problem because even though they outnumbered me, I was much stronger than four drunken girls and their sober friend. Reagan would obviously be the first to go, and the others would be too confused by what was happening at first to try and escape. And if they tried to get away or hide from me, there really wouldn't be a place where I wouldn't be able to find them.

The closer we got to the broken door, the calmer I felt. And while I was readying myself for any resistance, I also reveled in the fact I knew that no matter what, they just couldn't get away from me.

"Where's your house?" Larissa asked, stumbling over her feet.

"Right there," I replied with a nod toward

the half standing structure.

"What's wrong with it?" she asked, with a hiccup.

"Yeah, it looks like it's about to fall down," one of the others, whose name I had not asked, chimed in.

"It's fine. Perfect, actually. There's no safer place in all of the Ward," I replied as I approached the front door. I gave a glance over my shoulder to make sure they were still behind me and sighed when I saw that Reagan was still standing a few feet away, eyeing my home critically.

"Um, I think I'll just wait out here for everyone," she said nervously.

"Suit yourself," I replied as I pushed the door open. "I'm sure the wild dogs won't bother you."

When I heard her footsteps quickly approaching, I shook my head and scoffed quietly. The dogs in the neighborhood weren't a bother to me; I fed them whatever fat I couldn't sell or get rid of. As for the martyrs who didn't achieve sainthood, I would toss them their bones.

"What's that smell?" she asked, putting a hand to her nose. I stepped back to let her walk past me before securing the door back in place.

"We don't exactly get the garbage men out here, so I burn what I need to get rid of," I explained simply.

She nodded, unconvinced of what I had just said to her. I didn't give a shit at this point; I had the five of them where I wanted them, and now I had to get to work. I would have a long afternoon and night ahead of me, and I needed to get back to Emily before she came looking for me.

"So, where's the moonshine?" she asked, walking around my living room.

"One moment," I replied, leaving the room. I wasn't worried about her trying to leave because my door was a little tricky to open from the inside out, and the way I had pushed it closed assured that only I would be able to get it open again.

I went into the kitchen and pulled my shirt off. I let it fall on the floor next to my old, dirty refrigerator and reached up to grab the mason jar off of the top of it. I twisted the lid off and went over to the only cupboard that still had a door on it and pulled out a small, white, ceramic jar. Once the lid was off, I felt around for the spoon in the cupboard, then dipped it into the powder, dropped three heaping spoonfuls in, and mixed it before closing the mason jar up.

I was never really a fan of poison, because the martyr would have to feel the pain in order for their process to count, but Reagan wasn't going to be a martyr, so it didn't matter to me.

I was actually fascinated to see how quickly this dosage of arsenic would affect her. Once her organs started to shut down and her body turned against her, I would begin.

But first, I have to convince her to drink it, I thought, holding up the jar to make sure that no traces of the poison were floating about.

I reached down and picked up my shirt, tossing it onto the counter, before I went back into the living room, jar in hand. I found the five of them sitting in a semi-circle chatting away, except for Reagan, who seemed to be meticulously looking over every inch of the room.

"As promised," I said, handing her the jar and sitting down next to Larissa. I had to make sure that she didn't drink the moonshine, or she would be damaged goods and a waste of salt.

"You lose your shirt or something?" Larissa asked with a giggle.

I glanced at her and forced a smile onto my face, "It gets hot in here quickly. I like to be prepared for the heat."

I waited while Reagan started to drink

from the jar. At first it was a careful sip; probably because it may have been her first time with authentic moonshine. The girls began to chat animatedly as Larissa's head ended up on my shoulder. It took everything inside me not to shudder at her drunken touch, but I did my best to successfully hold it together.

And then it happened. Reagan started to moan slightly, before she suddenly jerked back and dropped the mason jar onto the hard, wooden floor. It shattered with a loud cracking sound as the arsenic-laced, pure alcohol splashed onto the living room floor.

I leaned back on my hands and watched Reagan writhe in pain, holding her aching stomach, and smiled at the tears streaming down her face. I wondered when the blood would follow; the ruby-colored liquid that would tell me she was actually dying.

Larissa and the remaining three girls immediately crowded around her, trying to help, asking what was wrong. I took that moment to slip away and go into my special room where I made my martyrs, where I elevated lost souls to sainthood, and began to prepare.

I rolled my barrel of salt out, because I wasn't sure how much I would need. Some souls were more tainted than others, and if purification by fire didn't work, then I'd have to pack the open wounds with salt and take away what was left with the proper ritual.

I undid the top of the barrel and tossed the lid to the side. I wouldn't start making my symbols yet, but I could at least be sure that the space was clean. I went over to the small table that sat against the back wall of the room and lit some incense and white candles, and finally grabbed a broom to start sweeping away at what might potentially have been left over from the boy. It bothered me that I never had a real chance to clean up when I was done separating his skin from his bones, and I knew that if their essence's mixed, it would be dangerous for me. Rot and decay had to be kept apart from the new skin and bone; it was an unspoken rule and I planned to follow it.

There was one time I wasn't careful and found myself in a catatonic state for four days. It scared the shit out of me, and I didn't plan to repeat the mistake.

"Where did he go? Someone, help us!" one of the girls shouted from the living room.

I wiped the sweat off my forehead with the back of my hand and put the broom back in the corner. I went over to the barrel, grabbed a handful of salt, and tossed it onto the spot where the boy had been, then left the room. The salt would be able to saturate and cleanse what I missed—if anything—and then everything would be ready.

I had plenty of time to let the salt work, because I still had to take them out back to purify them. I was about ninety-eight percent sure that I had enough pieces of wood to make as big a fire as I needed. I needed one last thing before I went back to the circle of now terrified girls. The one thing that I would use to begin the process and allow them to realize they wouldn't be leaving my home the same way they had come in.

I let my eyes wander around the room until I saw it—my ritual blade. As I approached, I felt a calm energy pass through me. It was the same feeling I always got before I transitioned martyrs into saints. The magnanimous feeling that told me this would be over soon, and I would finally be able to rest.

Eighteen

Emmie

Jeffrey was right.

The further down the street I walked, the more ominous the feeling that was starting to come over me. Was I scared? No; I was too angry for that. Was I worried? A little bit because I wasn't sure exactly what I would find when I saw Grimm.

The bad man kills people and rips them to pieces, the children had told me. Would he do the same to me? Had he done the same to James?

I had too many questions that needed

answering, and I was hoping that Grimm wouldn't be in his "wrong place" and understand that I didn't want to harm him. Hell, I didn't even want to turn him in; I just wanted to know what happened to James. I had every hope that he might still be alive, that the story the children had told me was all wrong, and they were simply trying to play some kind of prank on me.

Hope was all I had to hold on to when it came to Grimm; even when I was a young girl. I would always *hope* that I would see him at Old Algiers. I would always *hope* that I could bring him home and play with him in our huge garden. I would always *hope* that he would never forget me, and we could go back to being friends like we used to be.

But if he had changed as much as they said, as much as they wanted me to believe, then that hope was going to die, and I knew it. I didn't know if I would be able to handle the truth about Grimm ... if there was any truth to him anymore.

I wasn't sure what I would do if he

turned out to be what they said he was. *Would I be brave enough to try and stop him, or would I run away and try to get help?* If I did the latter and James was still alive, his blood would be on my hands.

I started to walk faster. I wasn't sure exactly where I was going, but once I reached the end of the street that would take me deeper into the Lower Ninth Ward, somehow, I knew I would find him.

Once I reached that end of the street I had been directed to, I stopped and looked around. It was almost like the Ward had been split into night and day. One side was partially rebuilt—I assumed as much as it could be for now—and one side was still in ruins.

If I were the bad man, would I hide in plain sight, or would I hide where I know no one would look for me?

After looking back and forth at either spot a few more times, I decided to head toward the ruins. Grimm always had a passion for things that were broken when we were younger. I can't remember how many times he had fixed his fishing pole or used the same damn line.

As I walked through the quiet, somber half of the ward, I wrapped my arms around myself. The fear I had felt coming down this way left me and was replaced with a morbid curiosity as I passed abandoned home, after abandoned home. Surely, I'd find him in one of these; but I wouldn't know which one unless I got brave enough to start looking through the windows.

Most of the houses were empty, while homeless people occupied others. I could tell they were homeless 'cause of how they slept so comfortably on the bare, wooden floors. *Maybe they're not so homeless after all,* I thought to myself with a small smile.

It wasn't until I reached the very last house in the furthest section of the ward that I found him.

I had walked up to the window near the side of the house because I was almost sure I heard someone screaming inside. I was scared when I approached, but then I got angry at how dirty the window was and how hard it was to see through it, so I looked around and found a rock.

I took a few steps back, pulled my arm back, and let the rock fly through the window. Even if he didn't stop what he was doing, and even if it didn't stop the screaming, someone would know I was there and maybe the sound of the broken glass would draw attention from the other people that lived here.

"Help us!" someone shrieked from inside.

I ran up to the window and gripped the pane, ignoring the pain of the broken shards of glass cutting into my palms, when our eyes locked.

He had a girl in his lap and a knife of some kind up to her throat, and he looked absolutely stunned to see me looking in at him.

"Grimm? What are you doing?" I called out. He looked down at the girl in his lap, then back to me again, before he picked her up and disappeared from view.

That was all the encouragement I needed to run toward the front door and start trying to push it open. I had to save that girl, no matter what the cost would be.

Nineteen

Grimm

The way she looked at me had actually shaken me slightly; it was the reason I had hesitated. But without Emmie's accusing eyes on me, I was able to get back to work. I could hear her banging and straining against the front door, but I knew she wouldn't be able to get in unless I let her.

I also knew that with Emmie here, I wouldn't have time to purify them all through fire, so I would have to defile the disposable ones to make them unworthy of the flame.

I had once made a male martyr who

before I transitioned to sainthood, I had cut off his dick and kept it for moments like this. Because I refused to sully myself with the pleasures of the flesh, I would use his manhood to do it. Marie had helped me with keeping it erect and usable after I had sold her his bones. She had some kind of secret recipe she used on it, and out of professional respect I had never asked what it was.

I had to move quickly though, because if Reagan died before I had the chance to defile her, then I would be nothing more than a murderer and I refused to hold that title.

I went over to the barrel of salt, grabbed a handful, then went back and made a circle around her. It was my way of letting *them* know that she wasn't an offering; she was nothing more than a sacrifice as thanks for having heard me so far.

On top of the highest shelf in my special room was a wooden box that was lined with what Marie had called, "a blessed chamois lining" to keep the severed dick safe and ready for use.

I first grabbed the leather gloves she had also "blessed" and put them on, before I grabbed the box and opened it. *Still good as new, I* thought to myself with a nod as I went back to Reagan.

"It'll be over soon," I said to her coldly, as I knelt outside of the salt circle and reached for her pants. I pulled them off, then her underwear next and had to turn my face from the stench. There had been more men in her than any of the others I had encountered, and the lingering smell that always invaded my senses almost made me sick.

I pulled her to the edge of the circle and pulled the dick out of the box. It took a few tries to pry her legs apart, but when I was finally able to, I shoved it into her. She let out a pained moan, but I didn't relent. I kept moving it in and out of her, waiting for the moment that her body would react; to reach the climax I needed before I knew I could stop.

But how long does this take on a whore? I wondered, as sweat started to pour down my brow. I hated doing this; absolutely detested it, because that's when the stench would grow strongest, and begin to attach itself to the walls in the room.

"Come on!" I muttered angrily as I continued the in-and-out movements. She was almost where I needed her to be; I could tell by how easily I was able to slide it into her now. She was wet with desire for something she didn't even really know was inside her, because her body was dying at the same time.

When she started to breathe heavily, when her agonized moans grew louder, I knew I was almost done. What I didn't expect was her to die immediately afterwards. I didn't expect her to cum and then take her last breath, but I was happy that it was finally over. I let it fall next to me outside of the salt circle, and I sat back on my heels.

I rolled my shoulders a few times and looked at Reagan, who had blood trailing out of her ears and eyes and chuckled.

"Don't ever say I didn't do anything for

you," I mocked.

I sighed and got to my feet. I'd skin her and take out her bones later. Her blood would be of no use to me because of what I had to do to her, but the rest I would be able to sell.

"Oh my God!" someone yelled from behind me.

Twenty

I turned around and saw Emmie had somehow managed to get into the house. When I saw the scrapes and blood on her arms, I realized she had probably climbed in through the window. Oh, but the look on her face as she realized what I was now ... I couldn't tell if it hurt me or made me feel more powerful.

"What did you *do*?" she shrieked.

"You don't belong here, Emily Thibideaux. You're in a bad place," I said to her in a low voice I didn't quite recognize.

"Grimm! What is this?" she asked in fear, as she began to back away toward the door.

"This is me. This is who I am. The boy you knew doesn't exist anymore. I tried to save you from this, Emily. I told you to stay away, but you didn't listen to me, and now you see me for what I really am."

"What ... What are you?" she asked, her voice shaking.

"I'm just a man searching for power," I replied, walking slowly toward her. "I'm what happens when you get chosen for a purpose that you have no choice but to fulfill."

Emmie's eyes widened in sheer terror when I quickly moved past her and swung the door closed. Now I would find out if I was meant to spare her or not; by locking her into my room with me. My special room where the spirits demanded sacrifices and I obediently obliged them.

"I make martyrs and saints. It's the only way to make sure that I'll never need or want for anything ever again," I said to her, as I walked toward the very small closet I had constructed, that sat next to the highest shelf in my room.

"Do you know the difference between a martyr and a saint, Emmie? Let me tell you. A martyr is someone who dies for what they believe in; don't matter what it is. If it's any belief at all and they choose death over not believing anymore, they become a martyr. A saint is something entirely different; something special. A saint is someone who is worthy, just, and pure. Someone who had done such a great thing in their life, that they deserved and earned the recognition for it. But there have been martyrs that I've had who didn't believe in nothing, so they die for nothing like her. If they don't believe in nothing, they aren't worth the salt needed to cleanse them and prepare them for sainthood."

By this point, Emily was in tears. She had dropped onto the ground, her hands covering her girlish, beautiful face. Her shoulders shook so damn hard that I could almost swear she would die right there if she didn't stop soon.

So, I did the only thing I knew I could do for her; I opened the wooden closet door. the creaking of the old wood causing her to sob even louder.

I reached in and grabbed my machete; the one reserved for the saints; the *worthy* ones, and then I walked over to her, crouching in front of her.

"Emily Thibideaux, my very best friend in the entire world," I said softly, moving her hands away from her face. She looked up at me with reddened eyes and tear-stained cheeks and I let out a sigh, running a hand down the side of her face. I used a thumb to wipe away one of the fresh tears that began to roll down her face, and I looked up into her eyes again.

"Tell me, Emmie. What do *you* believe in?"

Grab your FREE copy of What Lies
Beneath by scanning here:

*"The atmosphere is dark and ominous,
and there's seemingly no escape from the
monster. But the question is, who is the real
monster?"* – USA Today Bestselling Author
Ellie Midwood

About The Author

Yolanda Olson is a USA Today Bestselling and award-winning author. Born and raised in Bridgeport, CT where she currently resides, she usually spends her time watching her favorite channel, Investigation Discovery. Occasionally, she takes a break to write books and test the limits of her mind. Also an avid horror movie fan, she likes to incorporate dark elements into the majority of her books.

View Yolanda's books by scanning here:

www.ingramcontent.com/pod-product-compliance
Lightning Source LLC
Chambersburg PA
CBHW060447300726
48975CB00008B/2417